NORTH EAST of SCOTLAND LIBRARY SERVICE
MELDRUM MEG WAY, OLDMELDRUM

CODY, AL

Shannahan's feud

WES

419829

SHANNAHAN'S FEUD

Shannahan had always been a loner. He didn't take much to people. He just wanted his peace and freedom and God help anyone who riled him.

That's where the landgrabbers made a deadly mistake. They figured he was only one man against an army of hired guns. But Shannahan was more vicious than a wounded bear when crossed—and he wouldn't give up until he had slaughtered all his enemies. His thirst for revenge was unlimited . . .

SHANNAHAN'S FEUD

Al Cody

WESTERNS

First published 1950
by Quinn Publishing Company

This hardback edition 1992
by Chivers Press
by arrangement with
Donald MacCampbell, Inc.

ISBN 0 7451 4513 2

British Library Cataloguing in Publication Data available

WES
419829

Printed and bound in Great Britain by
Redwood Press Limited, Melksham, Wiltshire

Chapter One

"INFERNAL NONSENSE!" The speaker's double chin quivered with the violence of his emotion, his stubby legs beneath a rusty swallow-tailed coat were spread wide. "Why should they keep it? I ask you, what've the Indians ever done to develop this country? To deserve land like this? Lazy, shiftless loafers, that's what they are, always hunting or fishing, leaving the work to be done by the squaws. What would they ever have in common with a white man, no matter how long we pampered them? What I mean is, could you ever make one of them cultured and refined? Like those gentlemen there!"

His voice rose petulantly, accompanied by an unmistakable gesture. Sam Shannahan, thus designated as one of the cultured and refined gentlemen, had a grin as he glanced whimsically at his companion, likewise lifted out from the ruck for this fleeting honor.

"Hear that, Bob?" he chortled. "It's your good looks that get me included! True worth recognized at last!"

1

Shannahan's tone was purposely light, while his long stride lengthened. But already his companion was pulling to a halt, swinging back to face the speaker, his lean, unsmiling face tightening. His blood was one-sixteenth French, and ran wild and unpredictable. Like Shannahan, Bob LaFontise was quietly, even elegantly dressed in the style then in vogue, two thousand miles to the east. But a more keen-eyed observer than the double-chinned man would have detected that neither of these men was a tenderfoot, for all their appearance.

LaFontise stared, his glance taking in every detail of the speaker—his stove-pipe hat, rusty to match the swallow-tail, and set on a bullet head. The tobacco-brown side-burns which strove to pattern after the stain leaking from corners of a too-wide mouth. Short, paunchy but powerful, the speaker was none the less a commanding figure, as attested by the not inconsiderable crowd which listened to his diatribe.

"You were referring to me, sir?" LaFontise's words were precise, clipped. He stood, seeming more than his actual six feet, in offended elegance. "To me and my friend, Mr. Shannahan here?"

The challenge in his tone was unmistakable. The speaker paused, momentarily taken aback. Then he nodded jerkily.

"Certainly I was referrin' to you, Mister. Rees Hosty backs what he says. No need for you to get on your high horse, when I was intendin' to hand you a compliment. I was sayin' that no damn Indian could ever be like a white man, like you gentlemen, even if we kept feedin' the lazy loafers for a thousand years—"

"And to you, Mr. Hosty, I say that you are a liar!"

LaFontise's eyes were dark. "My friend Shannahan is a white man—*and* my friend! But I am not a white man, Rees Hosty! I am an Indian—one of those lazy blanket loafers who could never even be made to look like a gentleman, to whom you are referring!"

Sudden silence fell. Hosty's shoe-button eyes had the look of being held by loose threads. For a moment he goggled from one to the other, sensing danger. Then Shannahan took his friend by the elbow.

"That's telling him, Bob," he commended. "Mr. Hosty, I consider it a privilege to call Mr. LaFontise my friend. Which is something I would not do with just any man, be his skin white or red! On the face of the evidence, Mr. Hosty, I'm afraid you're condemned out of your own mouth. Good day, sir!"

Leaving the discomfited Hosty staring, he bowed again and walked on, LaFontise now willing. Momentarily his face relaxed.

"That was telling *him*, Sam," he grinned, and sobered again. "But what the blazes is going on here, since I've been away? Look at these crowds right on the edge of the reservation, and men like him shooting off their mouth—"

"There's always a lunatic fringe, just as much here on the reservation as back east," Shannahan said thoughtfully. "But let's not allow it to spoil the day for us. You promised to show me some of your country, Bob, and after four years back east in college—well, I'm homesick for room and pure air."

"We'll get horses," LaFontise promised, and led the way toward a livery stable, distant half the town's length from the train now rumbling west, which had brought them to Antelope.

3

But his dark eyes were unhappily busy. Everywhere the town, set at the edge of the reservation, swarmed with people—a riff-raff who had the look of being gathered from the four corners of the earth, who seethed with a restless impatience. Shannahan had seen such crowds before, as when men stampeded to a new gold discovery.

"This was a wonderful place, four years ago," LaFontise grumbled. "I'd never heard of Mr. Hosty then. Now it's like vultures swarming around carrion. There's something going on."

"I shouldn't wonder if you're right," Shannahan conceded. "But let's get away from town and forget it. We've got a vacation coming. My highest ambition is to lie on my back in the sun, or, for really strenuous exercise, tickle a trout from under a rock. I think I'm going to like your country, Bob."

"You couldn't help it," LaFontise returned enthusiastically. "It's paradise on earth—the hills of home!"

"Somebody made a mistake," Shannahan grinned, "Most Indian reservations that I've seen are sun-baked and desolate, the most cheerless, worthless ground that the government could find to foist off on its beloved red children." His eyes swept appreciatively to the clear-running creek beside them, to the blue, pine-clad slopes, holding up the sky ahead. "This is God's country."

"I suppose it was a mistake—from the point of view of such men as Hosty," LaFontise agreed. "One they'd like to rectify, if they could stir up enough trouble and find some way to break the treaty and throw it open for settlement."

"Reckon that's what he'd like," Shannahan conceded, and

4

his eyes darkened. "I've seen it happen, down in my part of the country. It was a flagrant violation of your people's treaty rights, but white men couldn't bear to see a lot of good land in the original sod, as God made it."

"And a vast improvement they made, I've no doubt!"

"I know how you feel," Shannahan agreed soberly. "It's only a tiny fragment compared to the total that once belonged to your race—but the government said that it at least was to be yours forever, and a man likes to hold on to his own."

"That's it," LaFontise nodded. "So far as I'm concerned, I could make a living anywhere, as a white man, and do well enough. In a generation or so I suppose the rest of my people could be trained the same way, and maybe they should—men have to change with the times or perish. But the older folks, who are here now—they were young men when they were herded back here on the reservation, promised that it should be their land forever. They were trained to a different life. But they've lived here and kept their part of the bargain, and they're too old to change. If men like Hosty make a fight to grab what's ours, I'll fight back! I've heard my grandfather tell about the treaty—he was one of the signers of it, making his mark. 'For as long as the rivers run and grass grows,' it promised. This was to be our land."

He fell silent, and Shannahan respected his mood. Like LaFontise, he too was of this country, though this was his first visit to this particular section. He'd been born in a covered wagon beside the road. Twice he'd spent a season trailing cattle up from Texas, the long road to Wyoming, which lay now to the south. Despite the last four years at college, he felt far more at

5

home, back in the saddle, than he'd felt in academic halls.

But school had been his mother's wish, so he'd stuck it out—even the three years after she'd gone, so that there had been nothing to draw him back to his old range. Memory of that dust-clogged air where, only a few years before he'd ridden wild and free, had been like a nightmare in the recesses of his mind ever since. Perhaps that was why he'd shied away from going back.

He removed his hat, and his hair glinted red in the sun. He was as tall and lithe as LaFontise, a man with an easy smile and the look of wide spaces in gray eyes, which the confines of class rooms had never been able to dispel. Now he had the instinctive feeling of having come home again.

"Something's going on," LaFontise said abruptly. "Those crowds, Sam. There were a thousand strangers in Antelope—and usually there aren't a dozen! And Hosty haranguing them that way! We should have stayed and found out what's afoot. Whatever it is, I'll give you ten to one, it's nothing good!"

"Maybe you're right," Shannahan agreed gravely. "But let's forget it till morning. We'll camp along this creek, under the stars tonight. In the morning we'll go back and assume whatever burden may be laid upon us."

"That's sensible," LaFontise nodded. "We need one night with clean air in our lungs. We'll go on and find my grandfather in the morning. He's old, and as wrinkled and brown as a frosted leaf, and he never did learn to write beyond making his mark. But for good old-fashioned common sense, and a scrupulous sense of honesty, I've never found the beat. He'd killed his

6

enemies in battle, before they marched back here to the reservation, and he'd ridden from Canada to Colorado, from Washington nearly across to Minnesota. But he hobbled his itching foot and has never strayed off the reservation since."

"I see what you mean," Shannahan said. "Though, considering what this is, and what's beyond it—well, I think he's had the best deal by staying."

"I guess you're right. I—whoa, boy, whoa!"

Both horses, jogging sedately, had shied violently. The next moment, controlling his own with the easy skill of a born rider, Shannahan was out of the saddle and into the brush which bordered the trail, with a glimpse of the creek just beyond. Then he was stooping above a sprawled figure in the grass.

"Lend a hand, will you, Bob?" he called excitedly. "It's a man—either dead, or mighty close to it. Looks like he's been bushwhacked—shot in the back."

A PINE ROSE tall and stately beside them, and aspen fluttered the last of golden brown leaves above the forest carpet. Some of those fallen leaves were a darker brown with the blood which had seeped from this man's chest. He lay, half on his face, right arm doubled under him, and the mouth of a wound where the bullet had entered was easy to see. As they lifted him gently, Shannahan saw that his right hand clutched the butt of an old army revolver, half drawn from the holster.

But the next instant he forgot that as the man groaned and he had a look at his face—white under its tan, fast draining of life as his blood soaked away. Shannahan's face went a matching color.

7

"Dunk!" he exclaimed.

Only one word. But much was in it. LaFontise turned his sharp glance from the wounded man to Shannahan. Then, not stopping for instructions, he pushed through the brush to the creek, returning almost at once with his hat filled with water.

"You know him?" he asked, kneeling.

"It's Duncan Hauswirth," Shannahan exclaimed. "He taught me how to ride, after my Dad was killed—how to use a gun—"

As Shannahan raised his unconscious friend, LaFontise held the hat to his lips. Some of the water ran into his mouth, more down his bloodless face. Then Hauswirth choked, coughed, and his eyes opened.

For a moment they were blank, then pain laid its shadows across the fluttering pupils. But as he drank again, incredulity and recognition came into his face, bringing back a faint touch of color, the wan ghost of a smile.

"Sam!" he muttered weakly. "Sammy, boy! Now the Lord be praised for His goodness!"

"What happened, Dunk?" Shannahan asked huskily.

Hauswirth's eyes moved in a faint, negative shake of the head.

"I didn't—see them," he whispered. "Whoever it was—but I can guess!" Grimness replaced the pleasure of recognition, anger and fear were a blend in his voice.

"Listen—Sam," he breathed. "It's God's mercy you came along. I'll talk—as fast as I can. I'm going—soon. But two things I must tell you. Another sup o' the water, if ye will."

They gave it to him, and offered no remonstrances. Both men

8

could see that he was holding on to life now by sheer power of will.

"You were always the friend o' the Indian, Sam—so was I, though I've had my brushes with them," Hauswirth went on, and for a moment his voice strengthened. "Two years I've lived here on the reservation—Straight Arrow and I have been friends since as young men we fought each other with guns! Now there's a devil's plot afoot to throw most of the reservation open for homesteading—a swindle and a steal!"

He drank again, rested wearily in Shannahan's arms.

"It's Gertney that's doing it—he and his shadow, Rees Hosty, aided an' abetted by Nick Duffy, the agent. I've raised such a stink they've killed me now—but you've come along! Promise me you'll fight those skunks to a finish, Sam!"

"I promise," Shannahan agreed huskily. "Rest easy, Old Timer."

"That eases me," Hauswirth confessed. "I believe—in God's justice. But men must be his instrument here—or the devil triumphs." He was silent again, panting, eyes closed. For a moment Shannahan thought him gone: Then he roused, his eyes trying, almost sightlessly, to find Shannahan's face.

"That's only—a part of it. You remember my girl, Sam—my little Dot?"

"Of course, Dunk. What about her?"

"Gertney's been after her—he's always hated me since he did me dirt. She was with me—and they grabbed her. I'm afraid—" his voice faltered, one hand groping blindly for Shannahan's. He took it in his own, bending lower.

9

"Yes, Dunk! he breathed.

"Find her," Hauswirth gasped. "I'm afraid—"

And on that repetition his voice trailed off. LaFontise, meeting Shannahan's glance, nodded slightly. His eyes suddenly misty, Shannahan eased his old friend back to the ground.

"Murdered," he rasped, and the easy good-nature was gone from his voice. "And his girl kidnapped!"

"I'd say it had all happened within the last hour," LaFontise said. "Here's where the killer crouched and waited as they came along. Then he shot—and when she ran to her father, he jumped out and grabbed the girl. There was a struggle. Then he got her on his horse with him and rode off. We can trail them."

Shannahan gazed regretfully at the dead man for a moment, then nodded. He had no doubt of the accuracy of LaFontise's deductions. The young Indian could read trail as he would a printed page, and Shannahan's own eyes confirmed the story.

"One likely thing is that the skunk won't be counting on pursuit, at least not yet," he agreed. "We can't do anything more for Dunk—not now, here. Best way is to follow her fast, I guess, like he wanted."

They swung to saddles and were off at a trot, where the trail they followed quickly left the path, heading at an angle into the deeper hills.

"You know the girl?" LaFontise asked.

Shannahan shook his head.

"I've known Dunk almost all my life, but somehow I've never met Dorothy. Of course, there were wide stretches when our trails didn't cross. Then she'd be away at school when I saw him, or something. I'd guess she's about eighteen now—and beautiful. I saw a picture of her, taken a couple of years ago."

"This Gertney—he mentioned that Gertney had hated him since he did him dirt! What about that?"

"They were pardners, back a dozen years ago. Gertney was just a young fellow then. Dunk had made a gold strike. He was always too trusting of his fellow-men for his own good. As I understand it, Gertney cheated him out of his share—which was considerable. Worse than that, he left him, as he figured, to die in the desert!"

"He sounds like a proper rat!" LaFontise grunted. "And now Gertney is mixed up in this about the reservation, with Hosty and Nick Duffy! We've seen Hosty! Nick Duffy is the agent in charge of the reservation. Seems to me I've heard Gertney's name before, but I can't quite place him—"

"I can!" Shannahan's tone was tight. "He's got money behind him now, and no scruples. One way and another, he's gone up pretty fast in politics."

"Politics! You mean—sure! Why, he's the Assistant-Secretary of the Interior!"

"Yeah. And the Interior Department has charge of the reservations. He's out here—and there's a plot afoot, treaty or no treaty, to open up this reservation for homesteading. No doubt of that. It begins to tie in."

"Looks like we didn't get back to this country any too soon, Sam."

"Looks that way. And this Straight Arrow—"

"He's my grandfather. Robert LaFontise, the 3rd, in our present line. Though I believe that if *his* grandfather had cared to go back to France, he'd have been a marquis, or something to that effect. I understand that he was Robert LaFontise the ninth, in his line.''

"This," Shannahan said, "is growing interesting. And the trail's freshening!''

"There's an old, deserted cabin about a mile from here," LaFontise remembered. "The sign is heading that way. Likely we'll find her there!''

Sam Shannahan had never been so accurate in his judgement of a man than in his thumb-nail sketch of Nillo Gertney, Assistant-Secretary of the Interior. A man with money behind him, and no scruples. One who had gone up fast in the game of politics.

There was a vast ambition in Nillo Gertney, a lust for power and money. He had been trained in a hard school, and now, at thirty-five, there were few tricks which he did not know.

He was, in common parlance, a political accident. In one way and another he had pulled strings and contrived to be appointed to his present position. Unquestionably he had ability and was able to discharge the duties which went with it. But even in the comparatively short time that he had held the post, he had proved himself a headache to the Secretary, who had taken a trip to Europe not entirely for a vacation from other things. Getting rid of an unwanted assistant, appointed like himself by the President, was not easy. A vacation had seemed to be in order.

Gertney had been pleased at his chief's decision. For the time of the Secretary's absence he was Acting-Secretary. Already as Assistant, he had made contacts and discoveries which promised to greatly increase both his power and his wealth. Now, with autumn well advanced and the threat of winter in the air, his plans were coming to fruition. So Gertney rode with a smile relaxing his broad face, humming a light tune under his breath.

More than one plan was nearing accomplishment. Less than an hour ago, an old score had been paid off. The wave of a hat from a rise of ground, added to the distant blast of a gun some time earlier, had told him that.

There had been no choice, he thought now, regretfully. He'd half-way liked the old coot who had once taken him in as partner, who had saved his life when he found him, dying of thirst, in the desert. Such a manner of cashing in one's chips was not pleasant, and a vague regret had lurked in Gertney across nearly a dozen years that he'd been compelled to leave the old fool to such a death in turn.

Then, only a few weeks back, coming here, he'd discovered Duncan Hauswirth living on the reservation, still very much alive, incredible as that seemed. Hauswirth had not even tried to get back the gold of which Gertney had cheated him. It wouldn't have worked in any case, but most men would have tried vengefully. Hauswirth, pious old Scripture-spouter that he was, had disdained. Money had never meant much to him.

But that gold had meant a lot to Gertney. From that springboard he had gone on, reaching for power and grasping it. Now he was in a fair way to put over a deal which would make all his former efforts seem petty. It had required a discerning eye and a scheming mind to see the opportunity where the average man would have suspected none of existing. Just as it would require unswerving determination to put it over.

Well, he'd taken the preliminary steps. Getting rid of

Hauswirth was one of the most important. Gertney had tried to hold out an olive branch, telling a plausible story of past events, which Hauswirth had promptly branded as the lie it was. He had as scornfully rejected Gertney's offer of repayment, either sensing that it was meant for a bribe, of that restitution would never actually be forthcoming.

Gertney's reason for attempting to placate his former partner had been double. Hauswirth had somehow gotten wind of his scheme to throw open the reservation to homesteading, and had promptly set up a mighty row. For a meek man where his own affairs were concerned, he could raise the devil when injustice to others roused him. He'd always been a stickler for justice, as he liked to call it, and had entertained the quaint notion that the backward races, such as his Indian friends, were entitled to be treated with the same equality of justice as the white man.

The old man's tongue had been caustic, devastating. It had become necessary, as a matter of business, to still its wagging, once and for all. If a man couldn't be bribed, the only other sure way was to kill him.

Gertney's second reason had been more personal. He'd remembered the old man's daughter from a dozen years before. The scrawny kid had become a woman of charm and beauty, with a touch of wildness to lend piquancy. Despite the fact that she had been schooled somewhere in the east, she was a naive little girl still in many respects. And it was quickly apparent to the sophisticated Gertney that she was as much impressed by him as he by her.

Certainly no other woman had ever attracted him as she had.

14

In turn, the prestige of wealth, of being almost a member of the cabinet, Acting-Secretary of the Interior, had made its impression on her. She had received favorably his offer to reimburse her father, had believed the story he told. Even Hauswirth's heated denouncements had failed to shake her.

By that time Gertney had reached what was for him a startling decision. To marry her. After all, she was beautiful, talented. She could grace any house, even in the nation's capital. She would add to his prestige, would help to silence some of the ugly whisperings concerning him. Definitely it would pay, from every point, to make her his wife.

Gertney wanted her and intended to have her, but her father stood in the way. Well, the action of this afternoon would simplify matters.

He'd chosen his man carefully for the job. A hanger-on of the town, ironically calling himself Goodman, who could be trusted to do anything for a price.

Goodman had killed Hauswirth, as attested by the gunshot, then the signal of the hat wave. He'd grabbed Dorothy, and carried her off by force, to the little, remote cabin selected in advance. Now, with Hauswirth out of the way, and his daughter properly terrified, Gertney would presently arrive to rescue her, thus earning her everlasting gratitude. It was a perfect scheme, one in which he could find no flaw.

A SADDLED HORSE stood with dropped reins in front of the cabin. It was a remote spot in a lonely land, the old log shack still substantial but beginning to show signs of decay. Its one window had been boarded over, the door stood ajar. Weeds grew under the window, but grass had crept back to the door where feet once had beaten a path.

Shannahan glanced toward his companion, and they dismounted, leaving their own horses back out of sight, then without a word, began to circle, to come at the place from opposite sides. As Shannahan neared the door he saw LaFontise emerge from the small clearing at the rear, and they reached the door almost together.

Shannahan briefly felt the lack of a gun. This man whom they were following was desperate, a killer who had grabbed a girl in turn and brought her here. There was little doubt that, given a chance, he'd shoot to kill.

But neither Shannahan nor LaFontise had carried a gun for the last four years, and there had been no thought in their minds of such a need, back at Antelope. The thing to do was use surprise, to move fast and surely.

His first glimpse showed them—the man and the girl, there in the middle of the room, the girl in the man's arms. A big, hulking brute of a man, who would give plenty of trouble, even without a gun, if given a chance. The thought ran in Shannahan's mind, and he moved fast. As the man swung, hearing him, he launched himself, hitting for the chin.

Always Sam Shannahan had been a good fighter, trained in a hard school. For four years, at college, he'd been on the boxing team, captain in his final year. He'd learned a lot to go with what had been an effectively rough and ready way before.

It was his plan to make that one blow count, and it did. The man was big, barrel-like in build, though with the rough grace of

16

a grizzly bear. Hard as nails, outweighing Shannahan by forty pounds, he had no chance. The surprise was complete. He took it on the chin, and rocked for a moment on his heels. Then his knees buckled and he went down, dazed, not completely out, but helpless for the moment.

Satisfaction coursed in Shannahan. Not in long years had he enjoyed hitting a man so much. Here he was not only starting to avenge the murder of his friend, but rescuing a damsel in distress. He paused, blowing thoughtfully on his knuckles, with the wry realization that this big fellow had a granite chin, and that bare knuckles were not like the gloves. Then he glanced, for the first time, toward the girl, expecting to see gratitude on her face.

What he saw was the muzzle of an army Colt, held in her hand, the round cannon-like aperture of it only inches from his nose.

She had produced the gun like a conjuring trick, and her eyes blazed angrily.

"You—you—" she stormed. "What do you mean by hitting him?"

Shannahan goggled, more amazed than he had ever been in his life. Dot Hauswirth was pretty, even in anger. The realization that Bob LaFontise was now lounging by the door, watching with amusement, did nothing to improve his temper.

"Why shouldn't I hit him?" he demanded. "Didn't you want to be rescued?"

"Rescued?" she repeated witheringly, but her glance grew uncertain as it wavered from his bewildered face to that of LaFontise. Then anger came back.

17

"What do you mean, rescue me?" she demanded. "That's what he just finished doing—from that horrible beast who kidnapped me!"

It was Shannahan's turn to stare. He saw that her explanation was genuine, but it was the last thing that he had expected. By that time, the gun in her hand was wavering, and the man was stirring, rising to an elbow.

"Mr. Gertney got here only about ten minutes ago," Dot Hauswirth added primly. "He thrashed the man who had kidnapped me, tied him up and dragged him outside. And then—and then you came," she added lamely.

Her words were far more revealing than she knew. Shannahan glanced sharply at Gertney. So that was the way of it! He saw the pattern, with what Dunk Hauswirth had told him, as plainly as if it had been sketched out.

"So you're Gertney?" he asked, as the latter got to his feet. Not waiting for a reply, he swung back to the girl.

"You're Dot Hauswirth, of course. I saw a picture of you, taken a couple of years back. We found your father, dying. He said you'd been kidnapped, and asked us to rescue you. We trailed you here."

Tears came to her eyes, and through that mist she searched his face and found the truth there. It was a lovely, piquant face, Shannahan thought, even in the twist of grief. Dark hair, a puckish nose and mouth. Something elfin, wild and remote as this remaining bit of wild country in a land being too fast tamed for his liking.

"You say Dad was—was dying?"

"He died in my arms," Shannahan said gently. "It meant a

18

lot to me, too. He's been my friend ever since I could walk. I'm Sam Shannahan," he added.

Plainly she had heard of him, and favorably. Suddenly realizing that she still held the revolver in her hand, she colored, then thrust it toward the watchfully silent Gertney.

"Oh, I—I'm sorry. Of course I've heard Dad speak of you, Mr. Shannahan. Here, take your gun, Nillo. He—he'd just given it to me," she added by way of explanation.

Proof that Gertney was a smooth worker was immediately forthcoming. He had said not a word up to now, contenting himself with getting to his feet, feeling tenderly of his jaw, and listening. Now he smiled and held out his hand.

"You've a swing like the kick of a mule, Mr. Shannahan," he said. "But I bear no ill feelings, since it was a natural mistake, under the circumstances. You say that Mr. Hauswirth was your friend?"

"He taught me to ride a horse and shoot a gun," Shannahan retorted, and pointedly ignored the proffered hand. "I've heard of you!" he added.

An ugly red stained Gertney's cheeks, and his hand dropped. That was a declaration of war.

Shannahan plunged ahead recklessly. "There was a big crowd in Antelope when Bob LaFontise and I came through, a few hours ago. I didn't like the tone of that crowd, or some things that they were saying about the Indians and their land. I've heard some ugly rumors that there's a movement on foot to turn the reservation over to settlement by homesteaders. If it's just a rumor, then you, as an official of the Department of the Interior, can set me straight."

19

Gertney glared. It was only for a moment, but he was hard pressed to keep the rage from his face, to maintain a smooth tone. Here, he suddenly realized, was a dangerous man—a man who might prove even more obnoxious than Hauswirth had been, and coming along just when he had counted real opposition as having been removed.

From the way in which Dorothy was looking from one to the other, he knew that she attached great importance to this. Here was a subject which he had hoped, at all costs, to avoid, until he had cashed in on her gratitude for this rescue. It was with difficulty that he kept his voice smooth.

"Certainly I can set you straight, sir, if that's the reason for your antagonism. There has been such talk, that I grant. As to the basis for it—" he thought swiftly, and determined that a part of the truth would be more convincing than a denial which everyone, including Dorothy, would know was false.

"I'll admit that there is some basis. The matter had been under discussion and consideration at Washington for some time. That is why I am out here, in my official capacity as Acting-Secretary. It may be that a part of the reservation will be thrown open for settlement. As a white man, sir, you and your friend will both appreciate—"

"I'm not a white man," LaFontise cut in. "That's the second time I've been accused of that today. I'm an Indian—of this reservation."

Gertney eyed him narrowly, disconcerted. He swallowed, went on uncertainly.

"No one would judge it, sir, by your dress or speech. Permit me to congratulate you on both. As educated men, irrespective

20

of other considerations, you will both understand that in this, our glorious Republic, we must always do things for the greatest good of the greatest number—''

"It isn't necessary to make a political speech," Shannahan said drily.

"I'm trying to answer your question, Mr. Shannahan," Gertney retorted angrily. "Do you want an answer, or not?"

"Several of them. How does it happen, when this reservation was guaranteed to the Indians by solemn treaty, to be held inviolate for them for as long as the rivers run and the grass grows—how, under the terms of such a treaty, can it be thrown open for settlement?"

Gertney glowered. "I believe some such phrase as you mention was in the treaty, sir. Despite that, the document was imperfectly drawn. If such a decision is made, it may be done legally."

Shannahan doubted that. But quite likely there was some loophole through which a man such as Gertney might squirm. "Whether that is so or not, Mr. Gertney, there are such things as moral obligations, both for men and governments. And while the treaty may, as you say, have been imperfectly drawn, I am confident that that was a result of ignorance, not intention, on the part of all concerned. I am sure that the Indians, in ceding certain of their hereditary rights in return for a guarantee of this land, entered into the contract in complete good faith. As a citizen of this Republic, I should hate to think that my own government did any less, or would ever do any less in carrying it out."

Gertney squirmed. "You're attempting an abstract discussion now, Mr. Shannahan. I wouldn't want to judge the motives or lack of them of men other than myself. I am merely engaged in this matter as a representative of the government.''

''That's what I understand,'' Shannahan agreed. ''You are Assistant-Secretary in charge of such affairs. As such, I haven't the slightest doubt that the ultimate decision rests in your hands. And that, if you recommend that a treaty, entered into in good faith, shall be honestly kept, it will be. Or that if you point out a way to break it and suggest that should be done, that the Indians will be cheated and the government of the United States made out a liar! So what I'm interested in is what you intend to do?''

Chapter Two

"YOU HAD our Mr. Assistant-Secretary squirming on a hook," La Fontise commented, grinning. "He did a lot of spluttering and talking, Sam, but I don't think he fooled anybody—not even Miss Hauswirth. And she was the only one he wanted to fool. He knew well enough he couldn't get anywhere with us."

"I was talking for her benefit, too," Shannahan conceded. "He had her hoodwinked to the queen's taste when we got there. I think we at least planted a doubt in her mind."

"And you planted a fist on his jaw," LaFontise chuckled. "But he's a slimy sort, Sam. And you've made an enemy—a dangerous one. If he figured he had to get Hauswirth out of the way, he'll have some more of the same thoughts about you, after yesterday."

"They'd better shoot straight the first time," Shannahan said grimly. "That man of his killed Dunk, and he was the best friend I ever had. It wouldn't have been quite so bad if Gertney had really tied him up and held on to him, so that we could have seen him hang.''

''He never put a rope on him, of course,'' LaFontise shrugged. ''If his hired killer was to be turned over to hang, he might decide to tell who paid him. Gertney dragged him out of the house and told him to beat it. And, since we know who he is, the killer will keep a lot of distance between himself and the law.''

''It's Gertney who's really guilty, anyway,'' Shannahan growled. ''And I aim to get him for that, before I'm through. If he'd done his own killing, in a fair fight, man to man, that would be one thing. But this way, and making a sneaky deal to try and pose as a hero in Dorothy's eyes at the same time—that sticks in my craw.''

''We're home,'' LaFontise said unexpectedly. ''Take a look.''

Both men pulled their horses to a stop. It was a breathtaking view. They had been climbing gradually for an hour, had topped a rise and rounded a turn, and now, viewed from between two century-old pines, a valley lay outspread below. At its edge were the reservation buildings.

This was an artist's dream. The houses were of logs, carefully designed and sturdily erected in a natural setting. A stream flowed through the village like a silver thread. Off in the distance were garden plots and green fields. In the other direction, cattle grazed. It was as near to the idyllic as Shannahan, with an instinctive love of beauty, had ever come. Or ever would, he thought, short of Eden.

They rode ahead. Others watched them, gravely, politely.

24

Here were blanket Indians, but here too were others who dressed as white men did, and worked their fields with sober industry. Shannahan doubted that there had been much influence for good since Nick Duffy had been appointed agent. He was, in all likelihood, an appointee of Gertney and a tool to his uses.

But the influence of dedicated, conscientious men was plain to see. Given good land, fair treatment, and a chance, many of the tribesmen had responded. LaFontise was an encouraging example of what could be expected. But such results, Shannahan thought, could come only from fair treatment. If men who had entered into such a treaty with honest intentions found that it was only a scrap of paper and themselves despoiled, kicked around, there would be little incentive to improve or adopt better ways.

"There's my grandfather," LaFontise said, and indicated a leathery but erect man, his hair only slightly streaked with gray, who was superintending some small task. He wore a blanket over an outfit of fancy beadwork, and Shannahan would have known without telling that he was a figure of importance on the reservation.

His face expanded in a welcome smile at sight of LaFontise, and he greeted him warmly, then shook hands with Shannahan. His English was good.

"Let us sit in the sun," he suggested, and led the way to a bench beside the house, where the wall made a satisfying back. "It feels good to my old bones," he added.

For a few minutes they talked of many things, concerning their schooling and briefly of Shannahan's background. Then LaFontise explained the happenings of the day before, going into detail about the part Shannahan had played.

"Now, what's it all about?" he demanded. "I hadn't heard anything about this homesteading business till we got to Antelope. But it sounds serious."

"It is," Straight Arrow agreed quietly. "I did not know, until you came, that Dunk Hauswirth was dead. He was my friend, too. My good friend."

He stared at the blue blaze of distant mountains for a long moment, then spoke softly:

"Like you say, this Gertney is bad—a devil. He is strong. A man who knows what he wants. To get it, he is like a mad bull, charging. As to our land, Dunk has talked with me. Many moons he worked to find out. He knew that Gertney was not to be trusted."

"Just how bad is it?" Shannahan asked.

"Bad. Gertney has the aim to throw open seventy-five thousand acres, reservation land, some day soon. For homesteaders. A hundred and sixty acres to each."

"Seventy-five thousand acres," LaFontise exclaimed, aghast. "Why, that would take well over half the reservation."

"Yes. All the best. Dunk told me Gertney also plans to take another ten thousand acres for ranch for himself."

"That would give places to something over five hundred homesteaders," Shannahan computed. "And there are twice that many in town right now, waiting for a chance."

"Each day more come, like flies to honey," Straight Arrow added. "They wait, to know when the day will be. Many more are close. Soon they are everywhere. They expect it to be open soon."

"But how does he think he can get away with it?" Shannahan persisted. "The treaty—"

"The treaty, when made, was honest. But he find a hole in it. Dunk tell me that, day before yesterday. He plan go to town then, try and stop it. But he never reach it."

So there had been vital need behind that murder. Shannahan waited.

"He not know just what hole Gertney find in treaty," Straight Arrow went on. "But Dunk say it give him right to act for government, to throw open reservation for settlers. Not legal, maybe. But what does that matter?" He shrugged. "If done, and land taken, they never be driven off again."

By nightfall, having talked with others, Shannahan was dismally convinced that the old chief was only too accurate in his judgment. Legal or not, if the thing was done and the land taken, the claim-jumpers, or whatever they might be called, could not be driven off. To do that would require an army and bloodshed. A long court fight would be involved. Once they had the land, it would be held, legally or otherwise. Always the story had been the same.

There might be a mild furore around the country if the truth became known, but that would do no real good, nor would it redress the wrong. Gertney, if sufficient heat could be brought to bear, might be forced to resign. That would be the extent of his punishment, and he had probably calculated it in his plans.

It was a bold, lawless deal, but it had been planned to the last detail and he was coldly determined to carry it out. He would stop at nothing, even at murder.

There was one weakness in the scheme. That some

27

determined man might so arouse public opinion at the last moment, or perhaps get in touch with someone of influence at Washington, as to threaten the plan before it could be put into execution.

"That's it!" Shannahan exclaimed. "He's Assistant-Secretary. The thing is to get word to the Secretary himself, to others of influence, and demand that they put a stop to it until the matter, can be looked into! Come on, Bob. We'll head for Antelope and get a message on the wire right away."

"This Secretary," LaFontise asked, as they rode. "What sort of man is he?"

"I don't know much about him," Shannahan confessed. "Though I've heard that he was a square sort. His having an Assistant like Gertney is what makes me wonder."

"My understanding is that assistants are not always the choice of their immediate superiors, where political appointments enter the picture," LaFontise said sagely. "At least, it's worth trying."

"We'll try everything," Shannahan promised. "I told Dunk I'd fight, and I meant it. I've a friend in Washington who has influence. Senator Reardon. We'll get him on the job, too."

LaFontise's eyebrows crawled like a humping caterpillar. "I never knew that you were a friend of Senator Reardon," he commented. "How do you get that way?"

Shannahan grinned briefly. "Reardon used to be a cowboy," he explained. "He and my father were good friends. I rodded a trail herd from Texas, north to his ranch, a few years back."

"That helps," LaFontise agreed. "It strikes me that we've taken on a man-sized job, where we'll need all the influence we can swing to our side. Senator Reardon sounds—''

Somewhere a rifle cracked waspishly, and the next instant Shannahan was out of the saddle and thudding to the ground.

LAFONTISE'S FACE went tight and hard with anger; then he saw that Shannahan was unhurt. It was his horse which had taken the bullet, plunging wildly and going down sorely stricken. Even that would not so readily have unseated Shannahan. But instantly he had comprehended that the lead had been meant for him, so had furthered the play by tumbling and sprawling, safely to the side of the dying horse.

The next instant, LaFontise was spurring recklessly in the direction whence the shot had come, some two hundred yards to the side and higher up. A crashing in the brush attested flight, and topping the rise, he was in time to glimpse a man on horseback being swallowed by more dense brush.

Only then did it occur to LaFontise that he had made an excellent target of himself, that he was unarmed in any case. He rode back to where Shannahan was on his feet, looking down at his now inert horse. His lips were tight. ''Well, they've started—and we've got to protect ourselves. Let's go on to town where we can get guns.''

Antelope still buzzed and crawled with humanity like a disturbed wasp's nest, despite the lateness of the hour. People were everywhere, the land-hungry and the money-mad, and studying those he saw with cold appraisal, Shannahan judged that for every legitimate seeker of land, there were two leeches seeking to prey upon him.

It was late autumn. Tonight there was a change in the weather from the perfect days which had marked this last week of autumn, a thin haze between earth and sky which made the stars dim and far out of reach, betokening storm. Cold crept rawly, so that men shivered and cursed with a premonition of what was to come. White frost would silver the land like snow at dawn, ice would fringe the ponds.

For the most part, the town was open for business. Their first stop was at a hardware store, where they purchased six-shooters and cartridge belts. Shannahan buckled on his own, and grinned.

"I thought, back last spring when I was given a degree, that I was past such lawlessness as this," he confessed. "But it gives me a feeling of being well-dressed."

LaFontise bought a rifle also, a Winchester 30-30. He liked a long gun, even as he had a distrust for a revolver. And the memory of the attack at sunset was strong. If such outrages became habit, he wanted a weapon which would reach all the way back.

In a little restaurant, presided over by a tired waitress, they obtained coffee and information, the latter consisting of the address of the station agent. It required considerable rapping on his door to bring him from bed, clothed in a long nightshirt and a mantle of injured dignity.

"Ain't the days long enough, that a man has to be bothered all night as well?" he demanded. "What's it now? There ain't no train out of here—nor in, neither—till afternoon tomorrow. So if that's what you want—"

"It's not," Shannahan assured him, and dazzled his eyes with a gold eagle which reveled in the glint of the moon. "We're sorry to disturb you, but if this would make up for the inconvenience, we need to send a telegram. It's urgent."

The agent's long face transformed like that of a hound dog's with floppy ears lifting. He accepted the coin, rubbed it testingly between calloused thumb and forefinger, squinted lovingly and popped it out of sight with a low whistling breath.

"Gents," he said, "That'll make up for a lot of sleep. Be with you as soon as I can get my pants on."

"This will be a long one," Shannahan warned, once they were inside the station and beside the telegraph instrument. A smoky coal-oil lamp gave light. "I'll write, and you start sending."

The agent's eyes widened at sight of the address.

"A United States Senator, eh?" he murmured. "I've heard tell that this Reardon is quite a feller."

"He is," Shannahan agreed. "Is your line clear?"

"Ought to be. Nothin' ever happens at this hour o' the night. Yeah, everything jake."

Shannahan explained the situation, bluntly but tersely.

"Immediate action required to prevent grave wrong," and he closed with: "Urge you to see Secretary at once. Let me know. Sam Shannahan."

They watched while the message was dispatched. Then the agent looked up seriously.

"She's off," he said. "And I don't mind confessin', confidential, that I hope you get results. I been here going on seven years, and I know a lot of the Indians pretty good. This thing is a damn shame, aimin' to steal their land right out from under them. But it wouldn't do for me to express an opinion. I'm a

31

public official. You think you can stop Gertney?"

"Reardon will do a good job of trying," Shannahan promised. "If the Secretary tries to put him off, he'll find he has a bull by the horns."

"Yeah. Well le'see, it's gettin' on to midnight. Be two o'clock, back in Washington. Means everybody'll be asleep there, and they won't disturb a Senator with a telegram. Guess I'll be safe in going back to bed till daylight."

He turned at the door.

"You fellers got any place to sleep?" he asked, then made up his mind.

"Reckon you're trustworthy. You can spend the rest of the night in here, if you like. Just don't show a light or nothin' to let others know about it. Otherwise I'd have riff-raff crowdin' four deep to get under cover."

They thanked him, and stretched on the floor. Dawn was barely in the room when the instrument began to clatter. LaFontise roused, crossed to it and touched the key.

"I learned this sort of thing years ago," he explained at the surprised look on Shannahan's face. "Maybe I'm a little rusty—it's Washington, all right."

He began writing, passing the sheets to Shannahan as the message came in. Senator Reardon had been deep in a game of poker when the telegram had arrived. Although bed could not charm him away from the game, the message had quickly done so. It appeared that he had been very busy during the remaining small hours of the night, making himself obnoxious in the eyes of various officials who hated to have their sleep disturbed, even by a United States Senator.

32

"Which would worry him less than a fly buzzing," Shannahan grinned.

Reardon was troubled. In Washington, he was known as the friend of the Indian. He had long been an advocate of more enlightened methods in dealing with them. He was particularly opposed to the administration of many of the Indian agents, whom he had characterized in a speech on the senate floor as too often either incompetent or dishonest, or both.

Rumors of what was impending, here in the west, had begun to seep back to Washington, he explained, but they had been hard to verify. He was shocked at the situation revealed by Shannahan, and was trying to do something about it.

"Routed out a custodian and had a look at that treaty for myself," he wired. "There. is a flaw."

And that flaw, it seemed, gave the Secretary of the Interior the power to do what Gertney proposed—to throw open the land to homesteaders. Certainly it had never been intended that way, but by a devious twist of meanings it could be so construed and interpreted.

"And if it's once done, and the land grabbed, it can never be undone," Shannahan muttered, going back over the old trail in his mind. "It's dishonest, possibly illegal, but enough of a loophole for Gertney. After he cashes in, he'll resign and be out from under!"

That was the conclusion which Senator Reardon had also arrived at. Now came the crux of his message.

"The Secretary is in Europe, which leaves Gertney Acting-Secretary, with full power to act, until he returns. Am cabling the Secretary immediately. Will keep you posted."

33

"He did say something about being Acting-Secretary, didn't he?" Shannahan remembered. "It shows he's planned this whole thing carefully. And he's doing it out here, in person, rather than back at Washington, where it would raise too big a stink. He's even cagey about announcing the day and hour, so that nobody can get anything on him in advance."

"Well, if a message comes back from the Secretary, this morning, forbidding him to take action, then he'd face criminal prosecution if he went ahead," LaFontise pointed out. "Let's hope, that the Secretary is the right sort, or that Reardon can bring enough pressure to bear on him."

The instrument was silent now, and there was nothing to do but wait. Then, just as they saw the agent coming, it started again, and LaFontise took the message.

"There's the blazes to pay, Sam. Heavy storms over the Atlantic, the cable broken. Can't reach the Secretary. Congress not in session, so can get no action there. Will keep trying, but not much I can do till I can reach Secretary. Keep me posted. REARDON."

THE NOTES of the bugle rang clear and sharp across the frosty air, the lines in blue stood rigidly at attention as the flag climbed the lonely finger of pole and shook itself loose in the steady wind which blew, this morning, from the East. There was a glint of sun, as if in token to the fair day normally promised by a night of frost. But the haze of evening was building about the hills, and the sun was transient in its glory. The promise of storm had changed to threat.

From the window of his own sparse office, Major Michael McLeod, commandant, stared out as the flag went up, and his mouth drew to a thin hard line. By rights, he should be out there for this ceremony, as he almost invariably was. But this morning he had curtly delegated his second in command, Captain Fitzgerald, to the task, offering no explanation.

He might have explained that he was sick, which would have been only the truth. Sick at heart. It is not an auspicious beginning for the day to realize that you have been a fool.

For Mike McLeod, there was no alternative, no dodging of the shattering implications. He'd acted with the best of intentions, which, as he assured himself grimly, was no excuse. Now he'd done a thing which, at the least, compromised his honor. At the most, it might well wreck his career.

He swung about quickly as the door opened, followed by a quick, light step and the heady odor of hot coffee. He'd slipped away from his own house half an hour before, going as silently as possible, guiltily; aware that, as usual at this hour, his sister Kate was busy in the kitchen, preparing breakfast. He'd felt that a bite of food would choke him. Worse, he hated to meet Kate's clear, probing gray eyes, uneasily feeling that somehow she might surprise his secret.

She came now, carrying a tray with the pot of coffee, cup and cream and sugar, a fresh boiled egg, fresh rolls and jam. He returned Kate's bright good morning and eyed the repast guiltily as she arranged it on the corner of his desk.

"You're troubled about something, Michael," she told him directly. "But you need your breakfast. I've only brought you a

35

light snack today. Is it about this reservation business—the notion of throwing it open to the public for homesteading, regardless of treaty obligations?''

McLeod caught at that as at a straw. It had been worrying him, and it offered a logical enough explanation for his strangeness.

"Thanks, Kate, though you shouldn't have bothered," he protested. "Yes, I am worried. If it is thrown open—or when, for there seems to be no question but that it will be—we're in for trouble. There'll be ten men fighting for every available piece of ground, and the nine losers will be sore. Multiply nine by five hundred—" he shrugged." Not to mention the Indians, who are beginning to get stirred up."

"They have a right to," Kate sighed, perching herself on a corner of his desk and revealing a shapely ankle. She glanced approvingly at it, then watched to make sure that Mike ate his breakfast. The Major, aware of that, strove manfully to swallow. Seated so, Kate made a pleasant picture. Just turned twenty-two, she had been keeping house for him for the last couple of years, and those two years, he had to admit, were a vast improvement over others which had gone before.

Katherine McLeod was a source of constant wonder to her older brother. Gray eyed, her hair the color of an otter's sleek pelt, she was small, almost slight, but graceful as wind-blown mist, a source of inexhaustible energy. If she knew that Sid was in town now—but fortunately, she didn't.

"Isn't there anything that can be done to stop this Gertney from such a steal?" she demanded directly. "It's an outrage—dishonest, mean. You're the commandant of the army here."

"Which makes me just a policeman, with a job that I don't like," McLeod reminded her. "I have no authority over the Department of the Interior, certainly not in conflict with the Acting-Secretary. If Mr. Gertney chooses to take action, all that I can do is to obey orders."

"You poor dear," she sympathised, and stooped lightly to kiss him on the cheek as she picked up the tray. "No wonder you're down-hearted. That's no job for a self-respecting soldier."

"No, it's no job for a self-respecting soldier," McLeod agreed, and smiled bitterly as the door closed behind her. *If I was even self-respecting,* he thought. *It wouldn't be so bad!*

Gloomily his mind went back over the events of the past few days, to the unexpected arrival of Sid McLeod. Sid was his half-brother, and always he was turning up without warning and when least welcome, the proverbial bad penny. Sid was as handsome, in his way, as Mike McLeod was somberly plain; as happy-go-lucky as the Major was austere. Sid was lovable, but he was a wastrel and a fool. And always he managed in some way to embarrass his brother.

There were seven years between them, just as there was another seven between himself and Kate. For all that, Sid looked to be the younger, and acted it. They had grown up together, Mike and Sid, years during which Kate had lived with an aunt back east, or been away at school. Kate had scarcely known Sid.

Both of them had chosen the army. Certainly Sid was gifted enough, if only he'd had some sense of responsibility. More than once, during his own swift rise, in which he had caught up to, then outdistanced Sid, Mike had managed to keep him out of serious trouble. Until there had come the time when, off at another post and on his own, there had been nothing that Mike could do.

At least, not much. Sid had been court-martialed and discharged. Mike had managed so that it had not been a dishonorable discharge, but that had been the best which his friends could conscientiously do for him. Sid should have had it worse.

In the intervening years, Sid had occasionally turned up, but never before here in Antelope. A week back he'd drifted in to town, along with the riff-raff which was clogging the muddy stream of humanity now awash across this lower edge of the reservation, seeking to burst the barrier and spread all across it.

Sid had been in town three days before Major Mike heard of it. Then the word had been indirect. But after that, things had happened fast. The evening before, a message had come—word which had taken the commandant out from the post, going quietly to one of the dives in town. Rees Hosty's big Powder Horn Saloon.

Muffled in a civilian greatcoat, the Major had skipped in at the rear door, as suggested in the message, going straight to Rees Hosty's sumptuously furnished office. There Hosty had awaited him, and, slumped in a chair, eyes blood-shot, his face strangely colorless and old-looking since last Mike had seen him, was Sid McLeod.

Sid had attempted the old, smiling bravado, but it had worn

thin. There was a look almost of terror in his eyes as he slumped back in his chair and watched the saloon keeper.

"It's this way, Major," Hosty had explained bluntly. The rusty hat was laid aside, but the swallow-tailed coat showed wrinkled and insufficient for the bulk it tried to cover.

"I guess I don't need to tell you anything about your brother. He's said that you'd want it kept quiet that he was in town, and we've played along with him." His smile was utterly cold, without humor. "He's playing along with us, too. For big stakes."

"Gambling, as usual, eh, Sid?" the major inquired coldly.

"I've had the devil's own luck." The whine was becoming more pronounced with the years.

"How bad is it?"

Again Rees Hosty's answer had been blunt.

"There was a game all last night. He was four thousand the loser. When it broke up, he said he didn't have the money. I'd been givin' him credit on his chips—he being your brother, Major. He promised he'd pay."

"And now he can't! All right, Hosty, I'll pay it!"

Hosty's eyes met his unblinkingly. "Maybe you can. If I get the money, and he gets out of town—we'll just forget that it ever happened. I know what a shock this is to you, Major. Me, I'm a reasonable man. It's not your fault. I'm a gambler. You can pay me when it's handy—just so it's not too long—"

He sidled around the desk, dropping his hand on the Major's shoulder with a familiarity which Mike would have been quick to resent under other conditions.

"A lot of things are happenin' in this country, Major, and a lot more are going to happen. My friend Gertney's seein' to that. There's times when it's nice to have friends. Like you bein' our friend—and us bein' yours, eh? Keep that in mind, Major, and if things go all right maybe we can forget all about that four thousand—''

Chapter Three

REES HOSTY was Gertney's man, openly and unashamed. He worked with and for the Assistant-Secretary because it paid. Not alone in cash, but in simple patronage. The Department of Interior was a branch of government, and Gertney had worked himself into control of its leverage.

From Gertney, Hosty had learned the value of a machine. That cost money, but it paid off in the end. Already it was beginning to pay dividends here. A hasty summons had brought no less a personage than the Acting-Secretary himself to that back office, where Hosty showed him a sheaf of scribbled papers.

"The agent at the station ain't no friend of mine," he confessed. "But he has an assistant, Jinks Gordy, who's a good telegrapher—when he's drunk. When he ain't in funds, I furnished the whiskey. So he brought me these that he found there this morning."

As Gertney started to read, Hosty added casually.

41

"Jinks didn't write that. And while the telegram to Senator Reardon is in Shannahan's writin', the copy of that one *from* the Senator ain't in the agent's writin' neither, Jinks tells me."

Gertney swung around, quick-moving for so big a man.

"Then who—what do you mean?"

"Jinks says he saw Shannahan and his Injun friend comin' out of there this morning. They must have waited for any message. I'd say one of them took it right off the wire, and that Injun—like he says he's proud to be—wrote it down."

Gertney considered that briefly for its implications, nodded, and read frowningly.

"This is a devil of a note," he grunted. "I was hoping there'd be no stir in Washington till I had an accomplished fact here. Fortunately, the Old Man's in Europe, and we'll be done before he gets back. That's a lucky break, though—that break in the Atlantic Cable."

"Yeah. But this Reardon—can he do anything?"

Gertney scowled, and shook his head.

"I don't think so. He has a lot of influence in Congress, and if it was in session, they might rush through some sort of a bill to stop me from taking action. But since Congress isn't in session about all that Reardon can do is fume and fret. The real danger is this Shannahan. He's a wild Irishman, reckless as most of his breed and spoiling for a fight. I don't know what else he can do, if anything, but judging by what he's tried already, he'll be damned sure to try something else."

"If we let him."

"Exactly. What were you saying about the Major?"

Hosty told him.

"I figgered there'd be complications in this business, and we could use him."

"You used your head there, and I won't forget that. Get him down here right away—no, wait. It would look funny, him coming to town to see you. We'll go call on him."

The Major saw them coming, and recognized their probable mission with a sinking heart. Once alone with him, they wasted no time in preliminaries.

"There's one thing I want," Gertney said, and made it clear in those words that Hosty was only his creature. "This Shannahan is a trouble-maker. I want him arrested and kept locked up—for the next few days. Out of the way."

"On what charge?" McLeod's voice was expressionless.

Gertney made an impatient gesture.

"Any charge that's handy. It doesn't matter. What does is to have him out of the way."

McLeod felt sick. Because he'd been a fool, he was to use his authority unlawfully to hamstring a man who dared oppose Gertney in this proposed rape of the reservation. Anger flared in McLeod, but he kept it carefully hidden.

"I'm afraid there'll have to be some cause for action," he said. "After all, I am not a policeman, in the ordinary sense of the word. I am bound by rules and regulations. Of course, if I had some cause to take action—"

"We'll see that you do," Gertney promised. "But we expect action on your part then." With that flat warning, he took his departure, Hosty nodding back over his shoulder. McLeod watched them go, hating himself.

He was aroused from this bitter abstraction, presently, by a

43

discreet word from the sentry, and then the prompt entry of Sid. The latter grinning, unabashed.

"I put one over on my watchdogs, Mike," he said. "While they were distracted about something else, I dusted out. Figured I'd rather call on you than be held as a hostage. Oh, don't get excited. I didn't tell anybody out this way who I am."

McLeod studied him, pondering. Gradually a plan took shape in his mind.

"There's a post wagon going out of here in half an hour," he said. "After a load of wood. You'll go in that, past town. Then you'll be well advised to keep going."

"That's all the break I wanted," Sid agreed. "Once I'm gone, you can laugh at them."

"You're not only without honor, but you're a fool as well," McLeod retorted wearily. "I'll be no better off. But at least I won't have to worry about you."

He personally supervised the departure of the wagon, and returned to his own house to find Kate bright-eyed with planning.

"We're going on a picnic, Mike," she announced. "You and I, now. I want you to show me some of the reservation that I haven't seen. I'm curious about it, with all the talk. I want to know what land they propose to throw open for settlement, and what is to be left for the Indians. It will do you good to get away for a few hours."

McLeod hesitated, minded to protest that he was a busy man, then he nodded. It would be good to get away for the day, and Kate knew as well as he did that the post would run equally well without him for a few hours. In addition, he could not be called

44

upon to do anything against Shannahan while he was gone.

Angry impatience surged in him against the man. Didn't Shannahan realize that he was only stirring up trouble for himself, trouble which might be serious and could do no possible good? McLeod hoped, fervently, that he might get that through his head and get out of town while he had a chance.

The sun was still obscured, but the land was clothed in beauty. Half the leaves had been snatched from the trees by the wind, but they danced in a wild abandon of color, and those that remained had been richly tinted. A clump of aspen, bright gold, showed between the green of pines on a hillside. The creeks ran soft and murmurous, muted silver under the red of willows. Ducks, themselves a myriad of color, streamed across the sky and dropped to disport in a beaver pond. A moose watched from the edge of a meadow and moved in majestic calmness.

"All that will be gone—if this is settled," Kate said sadly.

"I'm afraid so," McLeod agreed. "It's been a slice of the ancient paradise, and men like Straight Arrow have helped to keep it so."

"I wonder if this Shannahan can do anything to stop it?" Kate sighed wistfully. "He must be quite a man."

"I'm afraid he's tilting at windmills," McLeod answered impatiently. "Idealism is one thing. Being practical is something else."

They rode in a big circle. McLeod was familiar with the reservation. They could not compass all of it, but he picked out a course which would show Kate more or less of what she desired. Finally they topped a rise, and below them was outspread a land in abject contrast to what they had been following. It was as though a page had been turned in a book—turned from a richly colored picture of the horn of plenty, to a blank page.

"Is this a part of the reservation?" Kate demanded.

"Yes. The least desirable section. The land is poor—thin soil, either clay or alkali. Not much water, scant timber, little grass. About all that thrives here are rattlesnakes and coyotes. It just happens to be a wedge inside the really good land, and as such, no one had had cause to complain."

Kate eyed his sharply.

"But this is what they want to leave the Indians—just this wasteland?"

"That's about the size of it."

"Oh, it's an outrage!" she cried. "Something must be done! I hope this Shannahan succeeds!"

McLeod made no comment. They turned back, across to the lush lands. It was time to think about spreading their lunch and eating. McLeod gathered sticks and made a fire, close by a small stream, preparing to boil coffee. Then he stopped with an exclamation of annoyance.

"Somebody's coming," he said.

"I know how you feel, but after all, we're the trespassers here," Kate reminded him. "And there's lots of room—so far."

The others came in sight, five horsemen. Two white men, three Indians, McLeod catalogued swiftly. They seemed about to ride on past, then one of the white men swung his horse and came up. He dismounted without preamble and extended his hand.

46

"I presume you're Major McLeod," he said. "As such I'd like to talk to you. I'm Sam Shannahan."

McLeod stared, for once startled and off-guard. Hesitantly he shook his hands, turned then to introduce his sister.

"I'm delighted to meet you, Mr. Shannahan." Kate said warmly. "We were just talking about you, and the splendid fight you're making to save the reservation. I hope you succeed."

"Thank you, Miss McLeod." Shannahan found himself surprised that the Major should have such a sister. The day seemed suddenly brighter. Belatedly he remembered to intro-duce his companions—LaFontise, and three from the reserva-tion, including Straight Arrow.

"We were just having a look, too, so that I'd be a bit more familiar with the country," he added. "Would it be an imposi-tion if we join you? We have our own food."

McLeod would have preferred it otherwise. He was uneasily in the presence of this man, who didn't look like either a dreamer or a fool. It probably would be only a matter of hours before he would be forced to take action against him, Gertney and Hosty would see to that. Action which, as a man, he hated. If only he hadn't gotten himself into such a mess—

Shannahan and Kate were getting on famously. There was an added pinkness to his sister's cheek which McLeod didn't remember, a sparkle to her eyes and a lilt to her laugh. Bob LaFontise, watchfully quiet, made similar observations in regard to his friend. The picnic went off pleasantly, with fresh-caught trout added to the menu.

"You must keep us posted as to your progress, Mr. Shannahan," Kate told him as they prepared to return to the post. "I hope to see you soon."

Shannahan took a sudden decision.

"If you don't mind, Bob and I will ride in to town with you," he suggested. "We have to be getting back there anyway."

Again there was nothing that McLeod could say in opposition. Kate was pleased. She and Shannahan rode behind, finding much to talk about. Up ahead, there was silence between LaFontise and the Major. Only once did the former smile briefly with a jerk of his head.

It was evening, with a fine mist of rain in the air, when they sighted Antelope and Shannahan and LaFontise took their leave.

"This rain will thicken before morning," McLeod grunted. "We're in for a real storm, or I miss my guess."

"I think Mr. Gertney will have his hands full," Kate returned abstractedly.

"You seem almost as much impressed by Shannahan as he obviously was by you," McLeod suggested, attempting raillery.

Kate looked quickly at him, smiling from under her hat-brim.

"I don't know about his part," she confessed. "But I was favorably impressed by him. I like him."

McLeod shied away from the subject, fearful of betraying his own unease if he said anything. He had caught sight of a horse standing near his office, a horse from the town. Instinctively he knew that he'd find a messenger waiting from Hosty.

His orderly confirmed it. The fellow had been waiting nearly an hour. The go-between's glance was insolent, once he found himself closeted with the commandant.

"Hosty sent me," he said. "He told me to tell you two things, Major. One is that you ain't as smart as you mebby think you are, and that he don't like double-crossers. The other, growin' out of that, is that your brother was picked up this afternoon. He's under lock an' key now—and as to where, that's for the boss to know. He'll be kept as a hostage, to make sure you live up to your part of the bargain. And he'll be well treated just so long as you do carry it out. Any time you don't—"

He made a derisive but unmistakable gesture across his throat, then, with a mocking imitation of a salute, turned and tramped out.

NICK DUFFY eyed his visitor out of wide pale eyes which were lost in the pasty whiteness of a puffily fat face. He clasped hands across a progressively larger middle and rested one foot on an overturned demijohn. Cordiality had never been a strong quality in his voice, and it was weakened now by a chronic throat ailment which reduced it to squeaky proportions, much to his annoyance.

"I'm happy to see you, of course, sir. Always happy to meet anyone who has the welfare of my charges—um, our red brethren, at heart. I have given the best years of my life to their cause, Mr. Shannahan—because it is very near to my heart."

Specious coin, words, and cheap. Sometimes they paid off. In any case there was nothing lost. But he had a feeling that they would make little impression on this straight-jawed young man.

49

"Do you ever read the Bible, Mr. Duffy?" Shannahan demanded, whereat Duffy blinked suspiciously at him, taken completely off-guard.

"The Bible? Why, er—ahem, a noble work, sir. I admire it profoundly. Its lofty teachings—"

"That's what I mean. Somewhere in it is a statement to the effect that you shall judge men by their fruits—in other words, that actions speak louder than words. If you're really a friend of the Indians, why haven't you protested to Washingtin against this proposed steal of the reservation lands?"

Duffy waved protesting hands.

"You impute unworthy motives of me, sir. Likewise to the government itself. My job——"

"Might be in danger if you offended the powers that be," Shannahan supplied. "And pocketbook outweighs principle, of course. I had hoped, though not very strongly, that I might find an honest agent here. It seems the hope was vain. Good day, sir."

The gaze which followed him was bright with malignancy, but Shannahan cared nothing for that. He had known in advance that there was a scant likelihood of help from the agent. It had taken only a few words to see that Duffy, like Rees Hosty, was another of Gertney's creatures.

He had a trapped feeling as he stood, looking down the rain-washed desolation which was Antelope today. As the Major had predicted, the storm was increasing in intensity as it grew older. The streets, thronged the day before, were virtually deserted as the itinerant population were driven to any sort of shelter which might be found. Their smouldering rage would drive Gertney to speedy action once the weather cleared, if nothing else did.

But there was little question of his not taking swift action as soon as the weather provided a decent opportunity. Not only had he planned it that way, but everything, including Shannahan's moves, would be forcing his hand.

He had made his preparations. Half a hundred men, specially imported for the purpose, had set up tables of fresh raw lumber at intervals along one side of the full length of the main street. Behind these, on the day of the drawing, they would conduct what would amount to a virtual lottery. Ostensibly they were clerks, agents of the government on that day, under the direction of Gertney. The last at least was true. It was Gertney's scheme, and they would carry it through as he wanted.

Supposedly each land seeker would receive a number from a clerk, registering his name and other pertinent data in return. All free of charge. A drawing would then be conducted, and the lucky winners would be permitted to swarm in and file on the land, a hundred and sixty acres each. Since there would be perhaps half a score seeking each available quarter-section, this seemed the fairest way of conducting the matter.

With that, had the land been legitimately open and the drawing fairly done, Shannahan would have had no quarrel. But he had heard numerous reports of what was afoot. Already, for a price, usually steep, many numbers had been sold with the guarantee that they would prove to be among the lucky ones. Shannahan had no doubt that every customer with cash would be given such a ticket, regardless of how many came.

In that alone would be a huge profit for Gertney and his

minions. But it was unlikely that he would stop there. Probably none of these purchasers would get a lucky ticket unless they again paid a bribe at the final raffle. Having given a bribe in defiance of the law, they would have no recourse through that law. If they could find the man who had swindled them and take it out on him by force, that would be a different matter.

Shannahan understood the scheme, and had little sympathy for most of those who were willing to bribe and cheat. They would deserve to be cheated in turn. But the proposed steal from the Indians was another thing entirely. It was the thought of them which gave him the feeling of being trapped and helpless.

He had raised a row, but to what avail? Even if his authority might be doubtful, Gertney was going ahead, and once he had set those vast forces in motion, there would be trouble, and in the long run not only most of these whites but all of the Indians would be swindled. And what more could he, Shannahan, do to stop it?

Duffy had failed him. Gertney was clothed in the power of his office, and while he held that was formidable. If Senator Reardon saw no hope of shearing Gertney of that authority pending the return of his superior, what was to be done? Almost nothing.

"I'll have a talk with McLeod," Shannahan decided. "He seemed like a decent sort—and his sister certainly sympathises with us. If I'm lucky enough to get to see her, my time won't be wasted! And the Major represents military government here."

But that, Shannahan knew, was a slender hope. McLeod was commandant, but he wasn't likely to act without authority from his superiors, and that would not be forthcoming. If he assumed to do so on his own, he'd get himself in trouble.

"But if he's man enough, he might risk even that—and his job—to prevent such a ghastly wrong," Shannahan grunted under his breath. "In the long run he might even turn out to be a national hero—though I wouldn't bet on it."

It showed the depth of his despair that he would now turn to McLeod as a last hope. Securing his horse at the livery stable, Shannahan turned toward the fort, quickly getting wet despite his slicker. The creek, in the few hours since the storm had really gotten under way, had changed from a placid meandering to a roily torrent, carrying half as much again water as the day before. The ground was deep, greasy mud underfoot, with pools and puddles everywhere.

"Some storm," Shannahan muttered. "The only good thing about it is that Gertney can't act until it lets up. Even land-mad men wouldn't stage a staking stampede in this."

He rode to McLeod's office, passing the sentry at the gate without objection. Leaving his horse with the orderly, he sent in his name and was admitted.

It was a long, low and cheerless enough room which served the post commandant for office. Kate had sought to make it less austere by putting curtains at the windows, but on such a day as this much more was needed. A big, ancient heater, bulging above its nickled footrests, glowed with warmth, taking off the chill. McLeod, uncomfortably aware of what his caller would want to discuss, greeted him politely but not warmly, then waved him to a chair.

"Your business must be urgent, Mr. Shannahan, to bring you out in this storm," he suggested, and inwardly wished that

53

Shannahan had stayed away. Gertney would raise a row if he didn't arrest him.

"I'm here for just one reason, Major," Shannahan said. "To try and stop this steal of the reservation lands."

"But why come to me? I have nothing to do with that."

"But I think you do. You're the law out in this country—the only law there is around here. You represent the government of the United States, which has a solemn treaty with the Indians, guaranteeing that this land shall be inviolate for so long as the rivers run and the grass grows."

"I don't know about the treaty, Mr. Shannahan. That is in the hands of the proper department—the Department of Interior. The Acting-Secretary, Mr. Gertney, is the man you should see. I'm only a soldier."

"Gertney is Acting-Secretary, but he's the man that's putting over this swindle."

"Those are strong words—"

"This situation requires strong words. Here, Major, is a copy of a telegram which I have received from Senator Reardon. Read it. You'll see that he considers it just as much of an outrage as I do, just as much an illegal trick being put over by a swindler who sees his chance to do it. He makes it clear that, if Congress was in session, they'd mighty soon put a stop to it. Or that the Secretary of the Interior could be relied on to stop it if he was only in this country. In the face of that, don't you think strong action is required by somebody?"

"*I* certainly think so, Mr. Shannahan, and I'm for you a hundred per cent!"

Both men glanced up, startled. McLeod had been frowning at

54

the telegram, and Shannahan had been so passionately concerned with his argument that neither of them had heard the door open nor seen Kate enter. As sister of the commandant and his housekeeper, she was accustomed to coming and going between office and house without challenge. Now, however, McLeod started guiltily and eyed her with displeasure.

"This is an official conference, Kate," he said sharply.

"Then I'm glad I came," Kate agreed promptly. "In this case, as a citizen, I'm glad to align myself with Mr. Shannahan in urging that something be done. I'm sure he won't resent my interest."

"On the contrary!" Shannahan bowed deeply. "You're doubly welcome, Miss Kate."

For a moment they continued to look at each other, almost forgetting McLeod. But a knock at the door interrupted, and the orderly announced, "Miss Hauswirth to see the Major, sir."

McLeod hesitated, and now it was his turn to feel an uneasy embarrassment, coupled with a strange eagerness—both of which, he knew, did not escape his sister's sharp eyes.

"If you have no objection, Mr. Shannahan—"

"None in the world," Shannahan agreed. "I'm trying to do this to carry on for her father. By all means let her come in."

Dot Hauswirth entered, pausing uncertainly at sight of the others.

"Oh, I—I'll come some other time," she stammered. "I just wanted to see you, Major—"

"Pray sit down," McLeod entreated, and there was a quality of mingled eagerness and diffidence in his tones, strangely at variance with his usual assurance. He was on his feet to place a chair for her. "I'll be glad of your opinion in this matter, since you and your father lived on the reservation and he knew a lot about it. I—"

Again the orderly knocked. This time it was Bob LaFontise. The Major arched his brows.

"Your friend, I believe?" he said to Shannahan. "If you've no objection, let him come in. The more the merrier, eh?"

LaFontise looked surprised at sight of the girls. He turned apologetically to the major.

"Your pardon, Major McLeod, but I was really looking for Mr. Shannahan. They told me he was here. I have urgent news for him."

"Let's have it." Shannahan jerked out, and nodded briefly to McLeod. Kate leaned forward eagerly.

"It's just this," LaFontise explained. "Gertney had been quietly passing the word to his men that the drawing and filing will be held at high noon on the first decent day—probably day after tomorrow. The news will be all over town in an hour."

There was a moment's silence, broken by the drip of eaves and the beat of rain against the windows. Shannahan swung back to face the major.

"You know what that means," he said. "There'll be five thousand land-mad men trying to stake and grab five hundred claims. They'll use force to get and to hold! You'll be in on this, whether you like it or not."

Once again the sentry knocked. Scarcely had he announced Nillo Gertney than the heavy bulk of the Acting-Secretary shouldered into the room.

For a moment Gertney stood, dripping water. He radiated

56

force—sheer physical force, a brute of a man accustomed to taking what he wanted. Then he swept off his hat, bowing.

"This is an unexpected pleasure, Ladies. I had to see you, Major. There'll be certain duties which must be handled by the army—"

Only then did he catch sight of Shannahan as he turned and his face darkened.

"What the devil are you doing here?" he jerked out.

Shannahan was quick of temper, but, as LaFontise well knew, he could be urbane to the point of aggravation when it suited his purpose. Now he bowed, smiling.

"I was under the impression, Mr. Secretary, that I was having a conference with the Major," he explained. "But, since it seems to be an open house, far be it from me to object, if he doesn't."

Gertney was no fool; else he would not have risen to his present position of power. He knew that he was being mocked, and he was in no mood for that. He advanced to front Shannahan, ignoring the others, big feet planted widely, heavy chin outthrust.

"You'll do well to have a care, Shannahan." he warned. "It's come to my ears that all this stink you're raisin' is political, that you're no friend of the Indian nor ever were—any more than you were friend to Duncan Hauswirth. I strongly suspect that it was your finger on the trigger that sent that dirty bullet into his back—"

He was openly insulting, talking for a deliberate purpose, very sure of himself. Shannahan's hair was not red for nothing. Temper flared in his eyes.

57

"You're a damned double-crossing liar, Gertney," he roared, and stretched the Acting-Secretary on the floor with one mighty blow.

FOR A man who had been knocked full length on the floor, Nillo Gertney was in excellent humor. It had not been necessary to simulate anger in the next few minutes, for he was mad enough. But he had attained his purpose. Major McLeod, white-hot with rage at such an occurrence in his office, had done the only thing possible, promptly calling the guard and placing Shannahan under arrest. Gertney could afford to chuckle to himself. He could take hard blows as well as give them, and now he had the troublemaker where he wanted him.

Assault and battery would be ample, though the charge could be embellished if necessary. The Acting-Secretary had no thought that it would be. He had washed out opposition as the driving rain was washing out tracks in the dust.

Within the gloomy confines of the guard house, Shannahan's thoughts ran a dismal parallel to Gertney's. That had been a mistake, losing his temper. He'd played right into Gertney's hands. What he had not counted on was the promptness with which the major had acted, the almost obvious relief in his face at so good an excuse.

"I didn't think he was in with that crowd," Shannahan reflected. "Certainly his sister isn't. But it's plain enough where he stands."

If there had been any doubts, they were swiftly being removed. Each request that he had made had been systematical-ly denied. He had asked to see the Major; to be given a speedy hearing; to have a talk with Bob LaFontise; to see a lawyer, and finally, to be permitted to send a telegram to Washington.

He had been given to understand that he would be given a hearing all in good time. Which meant, of course, at the Major's pleasure. That he was now under military law, the offence having been committed on the post, and he was therefore subject to military rules. And that, again, meant that he would be held without privileges so long as Gertney figured that he might be able to bother. After that, with a reprimand and possible apologies, he would be turned loose.

It was a high-handed procedure, but Gertney, through McLeod, had the power to carry it out. And power was what counted.

The guard house was an isolated cabin set off by itself. This fort had always had a reputation for peace and orderliness, from its earliest days. Part of that stemmed from the stern measures adopted by the commandant in those times. There had been numerous trouble-makers for a while, chiefly red but with a good sprinkling of whites. He had dealt impartially with both.

That had made necessary a good-sized jail. It was a square, low-roofed structure, containing a score of cells, separated by a narrow corridor. The windows were small, the construction heavy, and there had never been an escape. Now the building was empty except for Shannahan and his guard, who spent most of his time at the office near the front of the building.

With rain pounding on the roof and the clouds lowering as though they had a grudge against the earth, it was half-dark even a mid-day. When finally his guard was changed, toward evening, Shannahan accepted the meal which was brought and peered out without much hope. Each sentry would have the same orders, of course.

"It's at least good food," he commented. "And I suppose I should be thankful for small favors."

"Eh? Now phwat the divil—" the sentry caught up his lantern and thrust it nearer, peering through the bars of the door, his broad Celtic face suddenly warm with interest. "Sure and I've heard that voice before. Is't yoursilf now, Mr. Shannahan?"

Shannahan stared back in equal surprise. Then he extended one hand between the bars, to have it heartily grasped.

"Casey O'Dowd!" he exlaimed, "Where did you come from?"

O'Dowd set down the lantern, released his hand-clasp and removed his hat, the better to run the fingers of his other hand through hair as red as Shannahan's and twice as wiry. An uncertain grin was on his face.

"Sure and that's aisy to answer," he confessed. "Not long after I saw you last—and the saints presarve us, Mr. Shannahan, how the time does run, that was near three years back—why, do ye see, I had mebby two drinks too many and in me natural spirit av gaiety it seems I spoiled the beauty av a couple av policemen. In me soberer moments it occurred to me that the country thereabouts had grown unhealthy, and I should travel for me own well being. In that frame av mind a man in blue pointed out to me all the glories av sun, moon an' stars, which he claimed was to be found in army loife. 'T was a liar he was, but I clutched at a straw. I signed up, and they shipped me out here,

60

and to make a long story short, here I am."

His eyes were anxious as he peered through the bars.

"And happy I am to see ye again, Mr. Shannahan sir. Though not in such a fix as this, ye'll understand."

His friendliness was warming. As he listened indignantly to an account of how Shannahan came to be here, and, knowing that he had a friendly auditor, Shannahan went on to recount how he had incurred Gertney's displeasure. O'Dowd shook his head.

"Sure, and was he not me commanding officer, and a good wan as such men in authority go, I'd be sayin' mane things about the Major," he sighed. "As for that Gertney now, 't would be pure pleasure to punch him in the nose. Ye'll understand, Mr. Shannahan, dear, I couldn't speak so free ordinary. But with this storm that's ragin', and we two alone in here tonight, who's to know?"

"I appreciate it, Case," Shannahan assured him. "I wonder if you'd risk getting in trouble for me? I wouldn't ask it if I wasn't being denied my ordinary rights, or if it was for myself alone. But the welfare of a lot of others is involved."

"Don't I know it? I was at another post a spell, and the way the Indians are treated there, most av their land taken away from them—it was a cryin' shame. As to getting in trouble, more than once ye risked that for me. If it's anything I can do, short av turnin' ye loose, which I can't—"

"I wouldn't ask that, Casey. But when you go off duty, if you'd hunt up the station agent and send a telegram to Senator Reardon, it would help. He'll move things if there's any way to do it."

"Sure and I'll do that," O'Dowd agreed. "Tell me what to say."

KATE McLEOD eyed her brother anxiously, while he ate his supper in a gloomy silence. They had quarreled, for the first time in the nearly two years since she had come out here to keep house for him. She had denounced him for his summary arrest of Shannahan, and his tongue had been sharp in answer. Now she had prepared the meal in unbending silence, and he was eating it in an equally offended dignity, staring gloomily out the window at the rain-wet blackness.

Watching him, it came to her that he was troubled about something—far more than the occasion called for. He was the Major here, a young man to have attained that rank and the responsibility of commandant. Usually he carried it lightly, but tonight it was a weight upon his broad shoulders. Her own anger melted in understanding, and she crossed to him, her fingers touched his shoulder lightly in sympathy.

"Something's troubling you, Michael," she said. "And it's not like you—what you did today. I've been thinking. Are you afraid of Mr. Gertney?"

He looked up quickly, startled, and then away again, but not before she had seen the quick flush. His denial was too quick and positive.

"Of course not! What makes you think that?"

"Because I've never known you to be unfair or unjust before—or afraid of any man or the consequences," Kate replied. "Now you're being all of that, Mike. Won't you tell me why?"

He met her eyes again, opened his mouth, and closed it grimly.

"You're imagining things," he grunted. "I have certain duties imposed on me, and as a soldier, I have to do them, like it or not. I'll confess I don't like this—but he assaulted the Acting-Secretary of the Interior. I have no choice in the matter. I-I'll let him off as lightly as possible, after he's had time to cool his heels and think it over. That may keep him out of worse trouble."

"You mean, that you'll let him go after it's too late for him to do anything to oppose Gertney's steal?"

"That's hardly a diplomatic way to refer to the activities of the government, Kate."

"Diplomatic or not, it's the truth, and I'm ashamed to think that my own brother is aiding and abetting a scoundrel in such a wrong! That's what you really mean, isn't it—to keep him locked up until the deal is over with?"

"Kate!" McLeod exclaimed sharply. "I'd permit no man on earth to talk to me that way—"

"But I'm not a man," Kate reminded him. "I'm your sister, and I love you—even if I am ashamed of you!"

The storm showed no signs of diminishing in the cold gray of another dawn. It still poured its torrents across a drenched and shivering land, and on the higher elevations the rain was mixed with snow. Shannahan stared gloomily out his cell window, taking comfort in only one thing. This was the grand-daddy of all storms, and if he knew anything about weather, it would continue for considerably longer. While that kept up, Gertney could not go ahead with his lottery and throwing open of the reservation. The weather was far too bad.

He was interrupted by the approach of the sentry with his breakfast, and saw, with quickening interest, that it was again Casey O'Dowd. He held the tray in one big hand, a fluttering sheet of paper in the other.

"The top av the mornin' to ye, Mr. Shannahan, dear," he greeted. "It took a bit av doing to get on juty here the now, but wan boy was sick, and grateful whin I made the offer. And I routed out the agent from the depths av his slumbers, which at first annoyed him, but whin he found out 't was for ye, he went willingly enough. And here's an answer back from your fr'ind the Senator."

He shoved the paper through, and Shannahan read it eagerly. Apparently Reardon was not only stirred, but was moving to renewed action.

"Your arrest and detention an outrage," he had written. "Am wiring the commandant at post to tell him so. Other news all bad. Atlantic cable still broken, and no telling when they'll have it working again. Also a letter arrived from the Secretary. Instead of coming home to attend to his duties as expected, the fathead is taking a trip into the hinterlands of Germany for some fool reason. So there's no chance to reach him now in any case. But this whole affair is getting my dander up. I'm taking the first train west to protest in person, and to give you a hand."

Knowing the Senator, Shannahan knew that fireworks would pop upon his arrival. Would he arrive in time?

Chapter Four

NILLO GERTNEY shaved before a cracked mirror in the Traveler's Hotel, the best hostelry which Antelope boasted, and dourly reflected that the place was well named. Anyone forced by circumstance to spend a night here would travel elsewhere again as quickly as possible. He had been compelled to endure it for a week, and from the present look of the weather, might be here for another.

"I'll make a real killing, this time," he assured himself. "So it will be worth the trouble. But nothing less would make it so!"

His eyes brightened as he reflected that he was to breakfast this morning with Dot Hauswirth. Her attitude, during the last few days, had puzzled and disturbed him. She had been virtually eating out of his hand prior to the death of her father. All the meanesses which Hauswirth could say about his former partner had only served to enhance her interest. It had taken those sly insinuations of Shannahan to set her thinking.

But his own blunt charges against Shannahan the day before

had, he hoped, implanted the proper seeds of distrust. At least, she had agreed to eat with him. With any luck, he'd erase all doubt of himself from her mind at this meeting, while multiplying those concerning Shannahan. Perhaps before the day was over he could persuade her to marry him. It would be better to move fast in every direction, now.

There would be a devil of a row before it was over with, but he'd counted on and discounted that from the first. Once he'd gotten what he wanted, he'd duck out from under by resigning, and they couldn't do a thing. Plenty of people, in the long run, would hail him as a hero, a benefactor to the country. Wasn't he arranging it so that some five hundred families would have good homesteads? Making good use of the land which was virtually wasted now.

Wiping his razor, Gertney turned at a knock on the door. His eyes quickened with expectancy at sight of Jinks Gordy. The telegrapher dripped wetness, but there would be purpose in his coming.

"I found out this morning that Shannahan sent another telegram last night—and got one back," he explained. "I thought you'd want to know."

Gertney fished a gold eagle from his pocket and handed it over.

"I do," he agreed. "But how did Shannahan get a message out? He's supposed to be locked up, out at the fort."

"Dunno." Gordy pocketed the coin, and produced a copy of the Senator's message. "All I know is, he did it."

Gertney read the message, frowning.

"So Reardon's coming out here, is he?" he asked, and

66

scowled at the storm. "And I'm held up by this infernal weather. How long will it keep this up?"

"Dunno," Gordy grinned. "I'm just one day behind the prophets. But the way it's soakin' things up, it'll be so muddy that a horse or buggy'd plumb bog down for the first couple of days after it quits."

Gertney understood what he meant. Homeseekers could not stage a rush to swarm across the reservation lands and set their stakes until the ground was drier. That would mean more delay.

"And Reardon will raise the devil, once he gets here," Gertney reflected. "H'm. Once he gets here. He isn't here yet.

"Keep me posted if anything more comes up," he instructed. "I'll make it worth your while." He turned then to go down to breakfast, reflecting that he'd have a word to say to the Major shortly thereafter. Either the soldier could keep his prisoner in close confinement, or he'd take him off his hands.

He made his way down a dingy hall, forced to step across sleeping men, then down a creaking stairway. The dining room had been cleared of sleepers, for his pleasure, but signs of their hasty eviction remained. The hotel, like most other places, was crammed with humanity. Men who were in town because of what he had set afoot, people who, wittingly or not, would all contribute to his coffers.

As such, Gertney welcomed their presence. But he was shrewd enough to know that tempers were shortening under these conditions, that, forced to inactivity while the clouds spilled wetness, trouble would soon be inevitable.

For the moment it was all right. They realized, grudgingly, that he could not throw open the land until they could get out to set stakes. But too much delay would turn some of their anger against him. He'd have to handle this carefully to avoid a real blow-up.

He waited a quarter of an hour before Dot Hauswirth arrived. There were dark circles under her eyes, the marks of tears. Which was only to be expected, but her greeting as he arose promptly to set a chair for her, was composed but reserved.

Beyond a few carefully inconsequential remarks, Gertney was careful not to press until the breakfast was well under way. It was the best which could be secured where money was no object, and, though leaving much to be desired to a taste of late years grown fastidious, it was not bad. Gertney knew the effect of good food. He looked up with an appearance of grave concern.

"This has been awfully hard on you, Dorothy," he said. "The best thing for you will be to get away from here, as soon as possible. Once this storm is over and I can complete my business, I want to take you back to Washington with me. That's where you belong, anyway."

She did not pretend to misunderstand him, or evade the question.

"You mean, as your wife?"

"Of course. What else should I mean? I've told you that I want to make up to you, as my old partner's daughter, for the things he suffered. God knows *I* didn't intend it so. I was half-dead when I stumbled out from the desert, and was told that he had died. I never knew otherwise till recently. But I've told you all this before—" he spread his hands, big, arrogant hands that could grasp and hold.

68

She looked at him, her eyes fathomless, and went on eating, saying nothing. Once she had seemed to believe him, despite her father's blunt charge that he was lying. Now it was increasingly plain that she did not.

"It would be too soon—much too soon to get married," she said tonelessly.

"But why?" he demanded. "Oh, I know what you mean, dear—so soon after his death. But you do need to get away from here, you need someone to look after you. You have no folks, no relatives. Only me. And I want to look after you—to do everything in my power to make up to you for what you've suffered!"

Her answer was like a dash of rain in his face.

"No. I'll have to wait—until things are cleared up."

He was being honest this morning as well, within limits. He did not pretend to misunderstand what she was saying. That she would wait to find out the truth—whether he was an honest man, or a liar and a killer.

"I hoped you trusted me, Dorothy," he protested.

"My father didn't," she said quietly. "And he knew you pretty well." She did not attempt to relieve the sting of that statement by explanation. "There's something else that might make a difference."

"What?" Gertney asked warily. He sensed the answer before she spoke.

"About the reservation. I feel as Dad did—that it's a grave injustice to the Indians to open it for settlement, breaking an honestly made treaty. As Acting-Secretary you could at least delay the whole thing—say for a few months. Until next spring.

That would give time for discussion, to get everything—more or less ironed out.''

Gertney cursed Shannahan under his breath. He had done all this, implanted these seeds of doubt after they had been almost smothered. And the devil of it was that there was no convincing answer.

"You don't understand," he said, trying to put a vast patience into his voice. "People out here look at me as though I was some sort of a king. I'm not. I'm really the servant of government. This has been decided on as a matter of policy. I was sent out here to put that policy into effect. I have no choice but to do so. It has already been talked over, considered, and the decision made in higher quarters.''

That was a lie, but it sounded good in his own ears. But he saw that she was unconvinced.

"That isn't what Father said, after he'd looked into the matter," she said tonelessly. And Gertney knew, in that moment, that his worst mistake had been in killing Hauswirth. It had solved no problems, for Shannahan had risen up in his place, and he was a far more formidable antagonist in such matters than the old prospector had been.

Now, dead, Hauswirth would continue to stand between them, his words a more profound gospel to his daughter. While Gertney stared, baffled, fighting down his anger, Dot stood up.

"Thanks for breakfast," she said. "Good-by.''

NEWS CAME, late that night, of a wash-out along the railroad, half a hundred miles to the east. The creeks had risen to raging torrents, slashing angrily at whatever stood in their way.

Casey O'Dowd brought the news to Shannahan.

"No more trains from the east," he reported. "Likely not for another week. Sure, and I hate to be the bearer of ill-tidings, me bhoy. But I figgered ye'd want to know."

"Thanks for telling me," Shannahan agreed, and turned disconsolately the few steps to his small barred window. Captivity was getting on his nerves, coupled with the depressing weather. This last news meant that the Senator would be stopped. He turned back to find O'Dowd grinning at him.

"I'm stickin' me neck out to tell ye that much," he confided. "And but for the dacency av the Major, sure and I'd be occupyin' one av these cells alongside ye."

"What do you mean?"

"I mane that the Major called me on the carpet yesterday at the middle av the afternoon. It seems he'd found out about that tellygram, and he was curious as to how it had got out. 'T was no good to avade. He told me I'd done it, and so I admitted and waited to take me medicine. But he's not so bad a feller, the Major.

" 'I take it, O'Dowd,' he says. 'That this Shannahan is a friend of your's?'

"Sure and he is, and one av the best, I concedes. Whereat he warns me that he'll have no more monkcy-business, but, barrin' that, he's not so mad at me. And l'aves me still on sentry duty here."

That evidence of humanity on the part of McLeod seemed merely to mean that they figured he was now completely dehorned. And who was to deny that they were right? Shannahan glowered out the window. The wash-out would stop the Senator from doing anything, and Gertney could act when he pleased, in so far as opposition was concerned. He heard the changing of the guard, not bothering to look up. Then a voice just outside his cell door caused him to swing quickly.

Kate McLeod stood there, peering in at him. The new sentry was just behind her, frowning uncertainly.

"But I tell you it's against the rules, Miss Kate," he protested. "The Major's orders are that the prisoner is to see no one."

"Nonsense, Harold," Kate said sweetly, and at the use of his name the sentry colored uncomfortably. "I understand the rules and regulations. And I'm not going to say a single word to Mr. Shannahan, since it isn't permitted. But regulations don't condemn a man to starve. I've baked a cake, and I'm sure he'll enjoy it. Shall I pass it through the bars, or would you prefer to do that?"

"Well—uh—seein' as it's you—and a cake—I guess you can give it to him," the sentry granted. "Don't see no harm in that. But no talkin'. Them's orders."

"Not a word," Kate agreed. "I won't even tell him what I've put in the cake for flavoring, but let him find out for himself. Ugh! Such weather! I'd like to go for a ride, from the edge of town beyond the creek, if it wasn't so dreadfully wet, and if I had somebody to ride with! As it is, I suppose I'll have to just go back and wait to see when there will be a change."

She was holding the cake through the bars, wrapped in paper, but studiously keeping her head turned to the guard and ostensibly talking only to him. Shannahan took the cake and backed to his cot, not opening his mouth. Still chattering lightly,

72

Kate followed the sentry back to the office and so outside again.

Once she was gone, the guard stretched on the cot in the office, a slight dereliction of duty permitted under these conditions. Shannahan broke off a bit of the cake and put it in his mouth. It was excellent. Kate McLeod was certainly a good cook.

The cake was long, not too wide, but it had risen high. Speculatively he broke it in half—and cast a sharp glance toward the sentry. As he had guessed, this cake was of a shape to hide a gun, and there was a six-gun inside, wrapped in paper. It was an old trick, which had perhaps succeeded because of its very age.

Inside the cake was hollowed out, the lower part having been cut apart and cleverly joined again. He saw something else—a note, pencilled in neat handwriting.

"As you probably know," it ran. "The railroad has been washed out east of here, so Senator Reardon will be held up. Gertney is getting desperate. He intends to go ahead tomorrow, regardless of the weather. I hope you'll find a way to stop him."

It was unsigned, but he knew Kate had written it. Shannahan stood up, stretching, yawning loudly. The sentry sat up and blinked suspiciously. Shannahan called.

"This is mighty good cake, mister. But there's more than I want. Come on and have a piece with me."

The fragrance was delectable, tempting. He had seen the wistfully hungry look in the sentry's eyes. Now he responded promptly. So long as the door was kept locked between them, there was no infringement of orders.

Shannahan passed a piece of crusty cake through the bars. As

73

the sentry came closer, it was to find his arm suddenly grabbed by the wrist, while a gun muzzle was poked within inches of his face.

"This is loaded," Shannahan warned. "Fish out those keys and unlock the door."

It was easier than Shannahan had anticipated. Leaving the sentry to occupy his cell, he helped himself to the latter's slicker, then stepped out into the storm. Men were keeping under cover as much as possible. Usual outdoor duties and drill had been suspended for the day.

There was a sentry at the gate. He had no suspicion until he stepped out to challenge, and the look on his face was ludicrous as he eyed a gun.

"I hate to do this," Shannahan confided. "But it will be better for you if I tie you up. Somebody will find you before long."

Remembering Kate's bright chatter, he headed for the edge of town where the creek flowed. The stream had become a roily river since he had seen it last, so high as to threaten the wooden bridge above. Back in the brush and trees stood a saddled horse. A well-wrapped pack was tied behind the saddle.

As he approached, Kate stepped into sight.

"I hope you didn't have any trouble getting here," she greeted.

"Not a bit, thanks to you," Shannahan agreed. Unaccountably he found his breath short, words difficult to find. There was something about Kate McLeod which affected him as strangely as it was pleasurable. "I—I hope you won't get in bad with your brother because of this, Kate."

"We're scarcely on speaking terms the last few days, as it is," she said. "But he's really not bad, Sam. Something is worrying him, dreadfully. If I didn't know how impossible it was, I'd say that Gertney had gotten some sort of a hold over him, so that he's forced to act this way, against his will."

"Gertney can bring a lot of pressure to bear," Shannahan nodded soberly.

"I hope you can do something—though I don't see what. If you can't—then, at least you're free. You'll find your friend, Mr. LaFontise, at the railroad station."

"Thanks," he agreed. "I won't ever forget—Kate. And I intend to do plenty."

"I thought you would." Her eyes were bright, sparkling with rain drops. Quickly she turned and was gone.

There would be pursuit, once his escape was discovered. LaFontise was waiting with another horse, and he grinned at sight of him.

"That girl's a brick, Sam," he declared. "She made that up and carried it out herself, then found me and told me you'd soon be along."

"She's the only one who could have helped," Shannahan agreed. "What are we going to do now to make it worth while?"

"I wish I knew." LaFontise shook his head. "I don't. But I do know that there'll be real trouble if this comes off the way Gertney plans. Despite the weather, people are still coming here, hoping to get a piece of land. They come from the west on the train, and they're pouring in by wagon, buggy, horse and mule back and on foot. Their tempers are short."

"I don't blame 'em."

"Nor I. But if thousands of land grabbers start swarming across the reservation, intending to take everything they can find—land which belongs to my people both by right of inheritance and by solemn treaty—there's going to be plenty of trouble. I don't like it. I know the situation well enough to know that fighting back will only make a bad matter worse and do no good. But, my God, Sam, if they start—I'll stand along with my people to do what I can!"

"That's why we've got to find a way to keep it from starting," Shannahan said grimly.

"That's what I mean. There'd be hell to pay. Gertney's no fool, and he realizes it. But he's given orders, or had them given to the Major, to keep order with the army. I tell you, it's bad."

"It's to be tomorrow, I understand, regardless of weather?"

"I think that's the plan. Something has panicked Gertney. He's past caring how bad a mess he throws others into, so long as he gets his."

"What about the weather?"

"My guess is that Gertney will get a break there. It'll stop raining this evening. It won't be too bad tomorrow. There's more storm on the way, but twenty-four hours of dry weather will give him his chance."

"Then there's just one thing to do, Bob. This can't be done except by Gertney. It has to be official to get by."

"You mean—?"

"If Gertney isn't there to start it, it won't roll!"

LAFONTISE PROVED an apt weather prophet. The rain

76

stopped shortly before darkfall, and an hour later the stars were shining. There would be a rim of frost at daylight, and the over-wet ground would be frozen hard enough to bear a man's weight in many places. This was all that Gertney had been waiting for. He announced that the reservation would be throw open to settlement at high noon of the following day, in a brief ceremony at which he would preside.

The word spread like a grass fire before a strong wind. A riot of emotions surged with the crowds, now beginning lavishly to patronize the saloons, already starting a premature celebration. This was the news they had been waiting for. Not only was it cause for celebration, but a few good stiff drinks might the better prepare a man for the tribulation which would begin at noon.

For, though there would be a crust of ice and the breath of winter with the new dawn, that ice would be gone before noon. And even the veriest tenderfoot knew only too well that there would be plenty of grief when the race got under way.

The booths of the harpies were well scattered, water soaked now. But they would be ready. Every man could draw his number at one of the booths. That should have entitled five hundred winners to begin a race for the most favorable locations, and a chance to stake. Even half a thousand racing men, each intent on getting the best, would make a fighting, snarling, give-no-quarter crowd.

But few among them were so trusting as to believe that only the actual number would receive lucky draws. Plenty of ringers would be put into the race, in one way or another. Others, even if they had no lucky number, would rush to stake, trusting to luck and a quick-trigger finger to hold what they had gotten, and to make an advantageous bargain afterward. No picnic was in prospect.

The old-timers, the wiser, and the better heeled, had come prepared, or had made such arrangements as possible since their arrival, some braving the storm of the last two days to journey to neighboring ranches below the reservation. Every available horse, mule, wagon or buggy had long since been purchased or leased at a fabulous rental. The town and surrounding country, up to the very borders of the reservation, resembled a huge camp.

Beyond that invisible line no man had ventured. Gertney had been as anxious about that as anyone, and McLeod had been determined. He had placed half his garrison on duty as soon as the word was given out, with orders that no man be allowed to cross and attempt to stake until the deadline.

"After that, it will be up to you to keep some semblance of order," Gertney added, and carefully got a long black cigar alight. "By the way, what are you doing about Shannahan? Have you caught him yet?"

"No. And I'm making no effort to," McLeod retorted, and some of the pent-up anger in him boiled to the surface. "I didn't connive at his escape. But since he's gone, I certainly can spare no men to try and hunt him down. Not with this other on my hands. And what difference does it make?"

"None, probably, now," Gertney conceded. He had the cigar drawing well, and took a few deep, satisfying puffs. "But he's a trouble-maker. If anything *should* happen—" he shrugged.

"If anything should happen, as you put it, Mr. Gertney—to

78

my brother, for instance, I could tell a story to the newspaper reporters who will be swarming here soon, which would make interesting reading. Don't forget that,'' McLeod warned. "I'm doing my part. I expect no less in return."

"I'll see to that," Gertney agreed. Inwardly he raged. It was lucky that he had a strong club to hold over this soldier's head, to keep him in line. He considered whether to voice a threat, and decided against it. Better not. After all, he'd pulled strings until an official order had come through from the war department, instructing McLeod to place his forces at his disposal, to keep order. That was enough.

He tramped back to the Traveler's, boots squelching in the mud, aware of the rawness of the air. He opened his door, and stopped suddenly at sight of Dot Hauswirth.

His eyes filled pleasurably to the warm rich vitality of her, the loveliness inherent in every curve and line.

"Dorothy!" he exclaimed. "This is an unexpected pleasure, my dear."

"I had to come and see you, once more," she said, and now she was close to him, looking into his eyes, her own pleading, her breath warm on his cheek. "I've come to ask you —please—as a favor to me, if for no other reason, Nillo, to delay this thing for at least a few days."

She had called him by his name, which had been rare of late. They had parted on a note almost of quarreling the last time. Now he smiled complacently.

"I'd do almost anything for you, my dear," he said. "You should know that. But as to this order—I've told you before that I am just an instrument for carrying out policy, which in this case happens to be orders. The department wants this done as quickly as possible, before the weather really gets bad."

"Meaning that you won't?" she asked.

"How can I? But I can do other things for you, and I will. You love this country, don't you? So do I. We'll have a great ranch—right in the heart of it here. You'll be a virtual queen—"

He stopped at what he saw in her face, the blazing scorn and contempt.

"Father was right," she said. "You're a liar and a scoundrel. Not content with all the rest, you expect to steal for yourself the best of the land, not even letting the homeseekers have a chance at it. And then you try to bribe me with that!"

She tried to get past him, to the door. Gertney grabbed her roughly, anger blazed in his eyes.

"And I suppose you aim to go out and tell people?" he asked.

"Why not?" You've got to be stopped, some way—"

"You little fool," he said softly, savagely. "Do you think I'm going to permit anything like that?"

"Let me go," she panted, and slapped him across the face. But again he imprisoned her hand, and now, at what she saw in his eyes, sudden stark fear leaped to her own.

"I'm not going to let you go," he said. "And don't try screaming, for I don't want to have to get rough. I'm not going to hurt you. But from now on you're going to do as I say, and don't make any mistake about it!"

Quickly he shifted both her hands so that he could hold them, despite her struggles, in one of his. She realized then that she was helpless as a child, that no one would respond even if she did scream, and so ceased to fight.

"That's better," Gertney nodded, but did not release his hold. He pulled her across to a what-not in a corner of the room, lifted down a small bottle and drew the cork with powerful teeth. There was a glass on his bureau, a pitcher of water beside it. He dropped a tablet from the bottle into the glass, poured it half full of water. The pellet swiftly dissolved.

"Drink it," he ordered, holding it to her mouth. "Drink it. Oh, it won't hurt you. It's a mild drug—I figured I might have need of it. But don't worry, girl. I'm not going to hurt you. Quite the contrary. Tomorrow morning I'm going to marry you, and as soon as you drink this, I'll call the landlady and have her assist you to your room."

She hesitated, looking into his eyes. But there was relentless purpose there, and she could do no other. Slowly she drank the drug.

This hastened his plans, but Gertney was smiling as he considered. After all, it was much better, the only good way. She would be like a sleep-walker the next day—able to walk and eat, even to talk a little, saying things submissively like a child when directed. There would be a vacant light in her eyes, but that would wear off within twenty-four hours of taking the drug. By then she would be his wife.

That was not only victory, giving him what he wanted, but it was absolutely necessary to his own safety, as he realized. Otherwise, if permitted, Dorothy would surely tell all that she knew, would openly charge him with her father's murder. Coming from her, that might prove not only embarrassing but serious.

But as his wife she could not testify against him. That risk was being nicely eliminated.

Otherwise, the event fitted in well. Everybody knew that tomorrow was his big day, and this would give it a fitting send-off, the wedding at ten, the opening of the reservation at twelve. He'd be kept busy, but it would work out. By evening, they'd be away from here, ducking out from under before the repercussions could begin. Once he had set the works in motion, nothing could stop it.

From a safe distance, he'd send in his resignation to the department, and while there might be a lot of indignation-meetings, what could anyone do? Most of those who would feel the strongest, being practical politicians, would know the answer, and presently forget it. After all, it was a game, and if he was the better player and raked in the pot, squalling would do no good.

"She's had a fainting spell," he told the solicitous landlady. "All this worry over the death of her father, you know. Get her to bed in her own room, I'm sure she'll be all right by morning. I want her to be, for we're to be married at ten."

He took pleasure in repeating that announcement so that the news would spread. It would give others a new topic to think about, which would be helpful. Any resentment at him would be swallowed up; likewise any suspicion of the past. If Hauswirth's daughter was to marry him, that in itself was an answer to many things.

There was just one fly in the ointment. Gertney went early to bed, pleading that he wanted to be fresh for the big day ahead. That sounded well, and not even to himself would he have admitted the truth. But he locked his door carefully shoved the bureau in front of the window, then examined his revolver and slipped it under his pillow.

"That damned Shannahan," he muttered. "Of course he won't dare to show himself around here again. But he's a wild Irishman, and those are the worst kind of reckless fools."

Chapter Five

THE NEWS of the impending wedding was a shock to the
Major. He knew the gossip, common in the barracks, that Nillo
Gertney had begun his climb to power by leaving his partner,
Dot's father, to die in the desert. With that earlier tale was linked
the suspicion that Hauswirth's murder was out of the same
bloody piece of cloth. Knowing Gertney as he did, McLeod
could well believe the gossip.

The thought that Dorothy would so callously marry the man
whom her father had hated, and do it so quickly after his death,
troubled him more than he cared to confess. It was as though this
news had suddenly shoved open a door in his mind which he had
kept stubbornly closed. Now it had let in the light, however
unwelcome. Revealing the truth to himself, that he hated the
very thought of her having anything to do with Nillo Gertney.

And the reason for that hate stemmed back to his own interest
in the girl. Mike McLeod had never been a ladies man, had
never considered himself as even slightly interested in any

member of the opposite sex. He had clung doggedly to that wavering faith so far as his mind went, even when it had been crumbling from under him.

He had encountered Dorothy on several occasions during the past months, and had come to look forward with a wholly unaccustomed eagerness to the time when he might see her again. Now he understood why, and with this news of Gertney the knowledge was a bitter pill upon his tongue.

Soberly he considered his position, and knew that there was nothing he could do. If she wanted to marry the secretary, that was her privilege. In any case, his hands were tied, and more than full with the new duties attendant upon the early opening of the reservation.

His thoughts went back to Sid, as they did many times a day. If it wasn't for him—the worthless, graceless scamp—then he'd throw off the shackles of that tricked debt and challenge them to do their worst. It might mean the ruin of his career, but there were bigger things in life. Men who had homes which they had always believed were their own, and who loved them as passionately as if their skin had carried a different pigment. There were other men who sought hopefully for homes in this same land. And who, McLeod knew, were mostly due for disappointment.

For himself, he no longer cared. But if he balked at doing his part, Sid McLeod would pay with his life.

Coming in to supper, Mike surprised a look in Kate's eyes which disconcerted him—a look of sympathy and understanding. He should, he knew, be angry at her for her interference in the affairs of the post. Had she been a man he would have taken drastic action. As it was, he had studiously avoided the subject, secretly glad that she had freed Shannahan.

"Are you going to let him get away with this?" Kate demanded, as she poured a steaming cup of coffee for him.

"Let who get away with what?" McLeod parried. "That's a pretty vague question, Kate."

"But your mind isn't so vague. You know who and what I mean. Gertney."

Wearily he set down his coffee cup and turned to her, like a little boy in need of mothering.

"Have you any suggestions? What can I do? I'm a soldier. My hands are tied."

"Do you have to leave them so?" she challenged. "After all, you are the commandant here."

"Which only makes it worse. I'm under order—"

"Orders which Nillo Gertney has presumed to give you, when he had no right to do so," she flashed. "You are in a responsible position, and that gives you a duty to the community. Why don't you wire the war department for instructions—and tell them what the situation is? The real truth. You could also make suggestions."

He considered that for a moment, at first without enthusiasm, then with growing hope.

"I might, at that," he decided. "It at least could do no harm. By jove, I will!"

He clapped on his hat and reached for his slicker, leaving his supper scarcely tasted, but Kate did not object. At last he was ready to do something.

He was back in a quarter of an hour, sinking dejectedly into his chair.

"No use," he sighed. "The wire's down somewhere —which is small wonder, considering this storm. It'll probably be day before it's fixed."

Kate opened her mouth, closed it again. She knew that further prodding was useless. The orders which had already come through had instructed him to assist the Acting-Secretary in every way possible, to hold himself and his forces at Gertney's disposal. In the absence of later instructions those would stand, and McLeod was a soldier. He was caught, and the knowledge that he had helped set his own trap did nothing to sweeten the pain of it.

Bustle and activity marked the day. Tired but eager men were stirring, with the thankful knowledge that the coldly wet and generally miserable conditions of the past few days and night had brought them to the threshold of opportunity. They moved about, seeking to find wood dry enough for cooking breakfast, casting apprehensive glances at the sky.

The hour of the drawing was swiftly approaching, and Gertney was furiously busy with a hundred last-minute details. Men were constantly coming to him with their problems, so that it had proved expedient to set up a temporary office in one corner of Hosty's Powder Horn Saloon.

Already, to save time, Gertney was dressed for the wedding, so that customers, slipping into the Powder Horn for a quick one, paused to blink and feast their eyes, though few had the temerity to grin. He wore a cutaway and gray trousers, with a top hat resting on the side of the table which served him for desk—a hat not so battered or rusty as the one which Rees Hosty habitually affected.

Hosty was even busier, as Gertney's right-hand man. He was all over the town, a trouble-shooter, coordinating, carrying messages, doing the leg work. He gloried in it, for it gave him a sense of power.

Both men had almost forgotten Shannahan, supposing that by now he would be well out of town and keeping out of sight. Since he had tried nothing during the hours of darkness, the danger was past, Gertney had decided. Certainly it would be hopeless to think of attempting anything now, with the town swarming with people who would be hostile to anything which might even threaten interference with the program that they were so eager to see put into effect.

A scant stone's-throw from his own doorstep, Hosty swerved from a puffing run at a hail. Here was a small building once used as a tool house and now abandoned, thought it had been occupied by itinerants the last few nights. Hosty swung around the door and inside, for he was constantly being stopped and consulted today. Many were fearful of going directly into the Presence.

"What you want?" Hosty puffed. "Make it short. I'm busy."

"This won't take long," said a voice which froze the grin on his face, and for the first time he twisted his head to look more carefully, in the uncertain light. It came as no surprise to see the gun in Shannahan's hand. He balanced it lightly, making a careless gesture which congealed the saloon keeper's blood.

"All that I want of you fits right in with your role of errand-boy," Shannahan added. "Now listen carefully, for if you make a mistake, it will be your last one. You'll go in to Gertney and say that one of the boys has collected a thousand dollars, but that he insists on talking it over with Gertney himself before he'll turn any of it over. Just that. Don't try to explain.

"Gertney will go with you. He'd swim the Styx to hell and back again for a smell of money. You'll take him straight across to that old blacksmith shop down the street, and inside. Do that, without making him suspicious, and you can live to die some other day. But I'll be watching every move you make, and there are other guns posted to keep you under cover as well. If you try to give any sort of warning, you'll be dead before it's out of your mouth! Now get moving!"

He prodded Hosty urgently in the ribs with his gun, and Hosty, eyes wavering in fascination between that steel snout and the coldly smiling face above, wavered on out to the street again. There was not the least doubt in his mind that Shannahan would do as he threatened, or that he could do it. From the edge of that doorway he could see Hosty go in to the saloon and up to the desk, and it was an easy gun shot all the way.

For a moment Hosty thought wildly of slamming the door shut as soon as he popped into the saloon, shouting a warning to Gertney. But he as promptly abandoned that as a notion as foolish as it was dangerous. The door stood wide, on the wrong side. To move to reach it would take only a second, but during that second he would be pitilessly exposed, and a bullet could move far faster than his own uncertain legs.

Hosty knew a moment of mild surprise at himself. It had seemed to him that the words must sound queer, coming from lips as stiff as he felt his own to be. But he said them glibly enough, and Gertney, beyond a quick flash of anger, seemed to find nothing surprising in the message.

"Damn!" he said, scraping back his chair and getting to his feet. "A thousand dollars—"

But it was the lure of the amount, already mulcted from the unwary, the need to keep such lieutenants in line, which impelled him. He followed Hosty outside, pausing only to clap on the stovepipe hat. He wore gray spats to match the trousers, and so picked his way with as much care as possible, following the soggy plank sidewalk, skirting the edges of a puddle which resembled a morass where the walk ended, looking distastefully ahead now that there was no more walk.

"How much farther?" he asked. "I'll be all splashed up!"

"Just to that blacksmith shop," Hosty assured him, and led the way. But his steps slowed uncertainly, as the enormity of the crime began to come home to him. He saw, suddenly, what this meant. If Shannahan got hold of Gertney, as he intended to do, he'd put a stop to the wedding and to the opening of the reservation at noon.

What he was doing was cutting his own as well as Gertney's throat. If Gertney went down now, great would be the fall. And in the ensuing debacle his props would crash along with him. They were at the corner of the shop now, but as full realization came to Hosty, he planted his stumpy legs and started to open his mouth, to grab wildly for his gun.

Could he have guessed the magnitude of Shannahan's reckless effrontery, Hosty would have revolted sooner. For the truth of the matter was that Shannahan had no men posted at strategic points to back his bluff. He was alone.

For hours, along with LaFontise, he had racked his brain in the hope of finding some plan which might stop or at least check Gertney. LaFontise had attempted to send another telegram, on the chance that there might be some new development at Washington. But the agent had informed him regretfully that the wires were down, not only to the east but also westward. Antelope was cut off from communication with the outside world.

The necessity of desperation impelled Shannahan to his strategy. The plan was so simple that he wondered why he had not thought of it before; probably that was the reason. The simplest ideas come hard. But when it had flashed into his mind, he had lost no time in starting to put it into operation, not stopping to count the risk.

Time was short; too short to secure any assistants. He gave LaFontise terse instructions, which he would just have time to carry out, without sticking around to do anything else. Then Shannahan made his way directly to the place where he had stopped Hosty. Since the streets were thronged with strange faces, he reasoned correctly that nobody would pay any attention to him if he went boldly.

Knowing men as he did, there had been no doubt in his mind

as to the reaction of either Hosty or Gertney. Greed and fear and the knowledge that there might be other guns covering them would do the trick.

Once Hosty and Gertney emerged from the saloon he followed not far behind them, until they neared the old blacksmith shop. It was at the end of the street, and brush and trees grew directly back of it and along the side. Reaching that cover, Shannahan plunged back among the trees and reached the shop just ahead of them.

As they passed him, Shannahan slammed his revolver barrel alongside Hosty's skull. At that, Hosty's knees buckled and he slumped to the ground, knocked cold. Gertney, puffing along behind him, started violently, jerked out of a not unpleasant reverie concerning the fruits of this day, fruits all ready to be plucked. But as he saw what had happened, he found the gun in his face, Shannahan's grim-smiling behind it.

"Keep coming," Shannahan instructed. "And keep your mouth shut!"

That had been close. But a glance at the recumbent Hosty assured him that he would raise no alarm for the next several minutes. Where he sprawled amid the mud and old weeds that had grown up during the summer, he was pretty well hidden from observation by any passersby on the street. Those who had camped in the shop during the night had abandoned it hours before, busily making preparations for the race to stake which would follow the drawings.

Gertney looked at the fallen man, back to the gun, and obeyed. He had no lack of courage, and he knew that his whole plan, perhaps his whole career, was threatened with ruin. Always a gambler, he'd take any chance which offered a halfway hope of success.

They plunged at once into the trees and brush, and these swept back in a straight line to the edge of the reservation, only two hundred feet away. There was no visible line at this point only the continuing trees, somewhat thicker now.

These were pine, a tall and stately growth. The soggy ground was carpeted with half-rotted needles which gave no sound. Gertney walked ahead, Shannahan behind—not close enough that he would be caught napping if Gertney should swing suddenly to attack, but in easy range to drop him if he tried to run. He had helped himself to a hidden gun which Gertney carried, and they moved now away from the town.

The ease with which it was done enraged Gertney. To be kidnapped right out of Hosty's saloon, from among hundreds of people, and not even an alarm raised! His anger caused him to check suddenly, swinging about.

"You can't get away with this, you know," he warned. "Not for long."

Shannahan's answer was chilling.

"Maybe not," he agreed. "But you'd better pray that I can. Because, if it comes to a show-down, I'll kill you before I'll let you go back."

Gertney's big hands had been working, closing and opening. Now they fell laxly at his sides. He had the conviction that Shannahan would do exactly as he threatened, and the fight went out of him. He turned and tramped ahead.

It was not far this time. All at once they were in a little natural clearing, and LaFontise was there, riding up on one horse, leading another. The strained anxiety in his face lighted at sign of Shannahan.

"You did it!" he breathed. "I was kicking myself, thinking of you trying that stunt all alone!"

"No trouble at all," Shannahan assured him, and his own face relaxed to a grin. He saw the fresh rage, coupled with incredulity, in Gertney's eyes as he understood.

LaFontise had brought two horses. Behind each saddle was tied a pack, containing supplies, and Shannahan had been explicit and particular as to the nature of those supplies. He knew that his friend had been full as busy as himself, to secure the necessary items, pack them and get here in the time allotted.

There were two heavy overcoats, a fur cap. Shannahan tossed the cap and one coat toward Gertney, shrugging into the other himself.

"Better put these on," he suggested, "You'll be more comfortable. Your plug hat is hardly suitable for a ride."

Gertney obeyed in grim silence. They were hardly half a mile from the town, but the noise of it was shut away as completely as the sight, so that this spot seemed like primeval wilderness. It would be easy to guess that there was no civilization within a hundred miles.

"I'd better go along," LaFontise suggested anxiously. "I'll get another horse and join you, Sam. You'll need me. This is a man-killing job that you're trying."

"If so, he's the one who'll get killed," Shannahan said, with an effect wholly for Gertney. "No, any more along would increase the odds, rather than lessen them, Bob. And you'll be worth more sticking around, watching, seeing what needs to be done and looking after it. Gertney and I will go it alone. Climb into that saddle, Gertney."

The Secretary obeyed, then, after a brief hesitation, put his hands behind his back at command, where Shannahan promptly slipped a rope about his wrists and tied it tight. The bridle reins he knotted together and looped over the saddle horn, so that he could drive the horse ahead.

A faint but unmistakable sound of wild yelling came as they swung away. Gertney turned his head.

"They've discovered what's up," he said. "Everybody'll be on our trail in nothing flat. You can't get away with this Shannahan."

"Maybe not," Shannahan agreed again. "Though like I say, you'd better pray that we do—if you know how to pray."

They moved at a steady, mile-devouring trot, a pace which the cayuses could keep up all day. Though he had of late years occupied a padded swivel chair, Gertney had been raised to such a life, and he noted how cannily Shannahan picked a trail. Taking advantage of every rocky patch of ground, of streams which could be followed, veering ever deeper into the wilderness, toward those rising, cold-looking peaks of the mountains. Not once, as they journeyed, did any sound of pursuit reach their ears.

"But you can't get away with it," Gertney insisted. "The army will take up the chase, and they'll have scouts who can follow a trail. You're just piling up trouble for yourself, Shannahan."

"Which you'll share with me," Shannahan promised. "You'd still better pray that they *don't* find us, Gertney—at

95

least not till after your boss has returned from Europe. We aren't on any picnic jaunt, but we're sure taking it, even if it leads straight to hell!''

"OH-H MY HEAD'S splitting! I think I've got a broken skull. I think I'm dying, Nick.''

Nick Duffy stared distastefully at his partner in nefarious enterprises. He had hurried to the Powder Horn, where Hosty had been taken, upon, hearing the news which threatened not only to upset all their plans but to spill a flood-like tide of ruin in its wake. He had never liked Hosty, associating with the saloon-keeper solely because he had to. The Indian Agent liked to think of himself as a cut above the average, and Hosty, at best, was only a whiskey-peddler.

Hosty mourned. "He half killed me.''

"Can't you get it through your head that we're in a mess?'' Duffy demanded. "I didn't come here to listen to how bad you feel, but to talk about what we can do. Shannahan's got Gertney, thanks to you. The crowd is boiling mad, but with the Major clamping down and threatening martial law, they can't do any more than tear a few places like this saloon of your's apart. That don't matter. What does—''

"What do you mean, it don't matter?'' Hosty sat up on the cot, clasping his head in both hands. "It matters to me, plenty!''

"Then, if it matters, we better do something. Things are at a stand-still, right now. But what's going to happen? Oh, why was I ever such a fool as to get tangled up in this with you and Gertney!''

"It was you and him got me into this, along with you," Hosty reminded sourly. "Well, I'm listening. What you got to suggest?"

"That's the trouble. I don't know what to do. But we got to hold things level till Gertney gets back. What can we do?"

"I don't think he'll get back," Hosty grunted, but he gave himself to the job of thinking. Their only hope, and he knew it as well as did the agent, was in Gertney's returning to take charge again. After some consideration, he decided it was not too hopeless.

"Shannahan's a wild Irishman, and mighty determined," he said, thinking aloud. "On the other hand, so is Gertney, and he's desperate. Likewise, there's the army, out looking for them, and a lot of other folks. The odds are not too onesided."

"That's the way I figure it," Duffy conceded. "*I'd* hate to be in Shannahan's shoes. If they catch him, he's in bad trouble even if it's the army. Kidnapping a government official, and a lot of other things. And if it ain't the army that gets him, anybody else will lynch him."

"Well, maybe Gertney will be back in time to do something," Hosty decided, and his tone was almost cheerful.

"That's what we've got to figure on. It's our only chance. If he goes down—so do we. But it's up to us to keep the situation under control till he does get back. How do we do it?"

Hosty got up, crossed to his desk, brought out a flask and took a stiff drink of whiskey. Color flowed back to his face.

"The only thing we got to worry about, right now, is if the Senator shows up," he decided. "I know him. Used to be a

97

cattleman, Morg Reardon did. Still has a big ranch in Wyoming. He's hell when he starts at anything. He'd raise plenty of it if he got here now.

"No need to worry about him," Duffy protested. "With the trains not runnin'—"

"I don't agree with you. It'll take more than that to stop Reardon when he gets going. So our job will be to see to it that he don't come bustin' in. That would finish us. But I'll tend to that."

Both the Major and his sister heard the news of Shannahan's exploit in kidnapping Gertney from under the noses of his crowd, with mixed emotions. Kate was frankly elated. She had been sure, all along, that Shannahan would do something if he was free to move around, and he had justified her faith.

Mike McLeod hid most of his thoughts. But one betrayed him.

"At least, there'll be no wedding today!" he ejaculated.

Kate looked at him sharply, and meeting her look, he colored uncomfortably. There was a new light in her eyes as she crossed to him and placed her hands on his shoulders.

"So that's it!" she said. "I'd wondered! You're in love with her, Mike!"

"I'm a fool," McLeod muttered. "Here she's agreed to marry him—"

"I don't think you're a fool," Kate said unexpectedly. "Dot has been rather acting like one lately, but she has fallen under the spell of glamor. After all, Gertney was straight from Washington, almost a member of the cabinet, and that sort of thing. It can be heady for a young girl, and he has a certain kind of charm. But I think she's been getting her eyes opened lately.''

''Then why would she agree to marry him today?'' McLeod demanded. Since it was out in the open, there was relief in talking about it. There had been so much which he was forced to keep to himself.

''I'm not sure,'' Kate said soberly. ''I'm wondering . . . about a lot of things. In any case, she'll be upset now and need a friend. I'm going to her now, Mike.''

''That'll be fine—only don't hint a word about—about this,'' he stammered. ''You understand—''

''Much more than you think I do, Mike. You're Major McLeod, commandant of the post, a soldier and a gentleman. But sometimes you're just a small boy. Don't worry about me. Your interests are safe in my hands. But what are you going to do?''

''What can I do? I have my orders—and a message just came from Nick Duffy, insisting that I use all my resources to rescue Gertney. I've nothing else to do.''

''I suppose not,'' Kate sighed. ''Though if he wasn't brought back, it would be better all around.''

''That's an outrageous thing to say, Kate, about an official of the government,'' McLeod protested. ''But in any case, I've no choice.''

''You won't be too rough with Sam—if you do catch him—''

''He'll be fairly treated, as would any other prisoner.'' McLeod swung. ''Don't you realize, Kate, that it'll be a whole lot better for him if I *do* arrest him? There are a couple of thousand disappointed homeseekers out after him, mad as wet hens. If they catch him, they'll lynch him!"

Her face went white.

"I hadn't thought of that," she whispered. "Maybe—maybe you had better get started, Mike."

It was her brother's turn to pause, studying her with appraising eyes. His own voice was suddenly husky.

"And so *that's it!*" he echoed. "That's why you've been championing him—even going to criminal lengths to set him loose from my jail! You're in love with the wild Irishman!"

Kate blinked through sudden tears, then swallowed and lifted her head.

"Maybe I am," she acknowledged. "But can you think of any one else who's more of a man? And after all, we're Irish too."

"God help us," McLeod said soberly. "Now I do have a job on my hands!"

Dorothy was awake. She walked like an animated doll, and even answered questions. But she seemed to be sleepwalking, and there definitely was something wrong. As a woman, the landlady did not like it too well. So she was more than relieved when Kate appeared. Since it was already past ten o'clock, and the Secretary was somewhere out in the hills on an unwilling journey, it was a safe bet, as her husband would put it, that there would be no wedding today.

"She acts queer, Miss McLeod," the landlady explained. "Like—like she was walking in her sleep. She don't seem to take any interest in anything. Even when I told her that Mr.

Gertney had been kidnapped, she didn't act like she heard me."

Kate took a look at Dorothy, spoke sharply to her, and turned grimly.

"She's been drugged," she said tersely. "That scoundrel! I'm taking her home with me!"

She did, without delay, taking Dot's arm and leading her down to the carriage which waited, with a soldier driving the team. Dot offered no objection, no comment of any kind as they drove out of town. Kate's first opinion was fully confirmed by the time they reached the post.

There she fed her guest, with stress on black coffee. But the results were disappointing. Dot answered questions mechanically, if they were completely simple. Otherwise there was a puzzled vacant look in her face, followed sometimes by a slow shake of the head. Nothing more.

"I'm going to put you to bed, my dear," Kate decided. "Maybe a good sleep will restore you. If it doesn't—" she compressed her lips, and there was a glint in her eyes which boded little good for the Acting-Secretary, if he should chance to return and seek to claim his bride.

"When I tell Mike about this, I think he'll be ready to deal with Mr. Gertney—not as the Major and the Secretary, but man to man," she reflected. "If he isn't, God help me—and if you've managed to do anything to Sam Shannahan, Gertney —I'll take a gun and kill you myself!"

There was one good thing about a wildly turbulent crowd. It was possible to move in and with it without attracting attention, and LaFontise availed himself of the opportunity. He was uneasy concerning Shannahan, but he knew that his friend was an excellent hand at looking out for himself. Right now, he had been given a job to do, and certain ramifications of it had begun to interest him very much.

There were some among the disappointed crowd who classed the Indians and Shannahan together, and who, cheated of what they had expected to have, voiced open threats of taking what they wanted, and without delay. But the presence of mounted, armed soldiers patrolling the streets and the border of the reservation, had a restraining effect. As did Major McLeod's grim order, that anyone attempting to trespass on the reservation would be arrested or shot.

That order had a double purpose. The Major suspected that Shannahan would be somewhere on the reservation, perhaps hiding out with the Indians, and this order would prevent the crowd from pursuing him. McLeod did not relish his job of hunting the man down, but it at least would be better than for the mob to find him.

Anger seethed and bubbled through the crowd. LaFontise went into the Powder Horn. The big saloon was crowded, the theme of anger a unanimous one. The door of Hosty's office was ajar, and he drifted toward the rear of the room, leaned somnolently against the wall. As he had hoped, voice drifted through—Hosty's and Nick Duffy's.

"He's showing plain defiance for you, Hosty," the Agent was saying. "Such an order on his part. I wouldn't stand for it. "Why don't you send word to McLeod that, unless he gets into this with both feet, you'll crack down—and hard!"

"Crack down? Me? How?"

"How do you suppose, you fool?" The Agent's tongue dripped asperity. "How did you and Gertney get a hold on him in the first place, except through his scoundrelly brother? You're holding him as a hostage, ain't you? Well, remind McLeod that he does things our way from here on out—or he won't see his brother alive again. Likewise, that there's a lot of mighty unpleasant ways for a man to die."

"Guess I was kind of forgettin' about that." The door closed then, but LaFontise had heard enough. So that was the explanation for McLeod's conduct. Here was a job which needed doing, and the sooner he was about it, the better.

Chapter Six

BY MID-AFTERNOON the storm had recommenced, here in the hills where now their trail climbed, and Gertney's last hope went out. So long as the air remained clear there had been a possibility that some of the searchers would follow and overtake them. Now, with rain sweeping so heavily that it was impossible to see more than a hundred feet in any direction, all sign would be washed away, and night and snow would conceal them completely.

Within a quarter of an hour, as they climbed, the rain had turned to snow, and Gertney realized despairingly what his captor intended. To head deep into those towering mountains, beyond the reservation, perhaps even to cross them.

Gertney had supposed that Shannahan would join the Indians, resting in comfort and shelter, trusting to them to hide him. But he was doing this the hard way, taking no action which would involve them in trouble. Back in these hills, even with hundreds searching, it would be a game of hide and seek in which the odds would favor the hunted. The prospect of plunging ever deeper into these fastnesses, where storm was king and winter already had laid a throttling grip, filled Gertney with terror.

It was not an unreasoning panic, however. Outwardly he remained cool, and his mind functioned. Any appeal was useless. Hope of rescue was a vain delusion. If anything was to be done, he must do it. Accepting that fact, he studied the situation calmly.

One of them would go back alive. It was in Gertney's mind that he would be the one.

It was probable that his fine plan was wrecked, his career ruined. There was still a possibility of getting back in time to retrieve all that he had aimed at, and he'd fight with that in mind. But even if he went back to defeat and disgrace, that was still life, and preferable to death. There was another and almost equally compelling motive for making a strong fight of it. He wanted revenge upon this man who had humiliated him, subjected him to such indignities as no other man had ever managed.

They camped, that night, in a gash of a canyon half way up the mountainside. The snow lay deep from the previous storm—belly-deep to the horses, so that for the last hour they had struggled slowly, through a blinding cloud of flakes so thick that it was impossible to see far past the rump of the cayuse. Mindful of that, and of the chance that his prisoner might try to fling himself off and escape on foot, Shannahan had tied Gertney's feet under the horse.

Now he released his legs, letting him down, and hobbled the horses. It had been a hard day for men as well as beasts.

105

Shannahan had made few stops. Neither of them had eaten since breakfast, and the creeping cold was in the marrow of their bones.

Here the snow was too deep to try and run on foot, even had his hands been free. Gertney did not consider it, nor did he complain. He made a short path, tramping back and forth, to warm himself as he could. Then, as Shannahan gathered wood from a windfall, he crouched before the fire, hungrily absorbing its heat.

Shannahan put on a can of coffee, sliced bacon into a skillet and dug out cold biscuits. A ledge of rock was at their backs, reflecting the heat, partially deflecting the snow which still managed to hiss and sputter in the blaze. Already the early dark had dropped like a curtain down the mountains, and beyond the firelight the flakes danced redly. Shannahan turned and untied the rope which held Gertney's wrists.

"How well you'll be treated depends on how you behave," he warned.

They ate in silence, wolfing the food with vast appetite. The coffee was black, scalding hot, doubly welcome that way. Shannahan took down blankets from behind his saddle and tossed one to Gertney.

"We'll sleep snug tonight, with this ledge sheltering us and the fire in front," he commented, breaking a long silence, "I'll make you as comfortable as I can. Roll up, then I'll wrap a rope around you."

Gertney offered no objection. That patience of his was a warning to Shannahan, even if he hadn't known already that the Acting-Secretary was a man of parts and no tenderfoot. But with the lariat wound three times around his arms, wrapped inside the blanket like a cocoon, he could not work loose during the night.

Shannahan took no chances, however. Two or three times he awoke to throw fresh heavy wood on the fire, for at this elevation the night air was not far above zero. Each time he examined the lariat, to make sure that his prisoner was still well trussed.

The next day they went on, ever higher. It was still snowing, but lightly compared to the day before. The storm was almost over. Since it was easy to see, Shannahan did not tie Gertney's legs. Now and then it was necessary for both of them to walk, floundering in the deep snow. It was not possible to see more than a quarter of a mile, and they saw nothing of any pursuit.

Gertney's hopes were rising. Shannahan was not getting careless, but the fact that his legs were free, even if his hands were tied, might give him a chance. And no man could maintain constant vigilance always at the same peak. There would be a let-down, a slip somewhere. When it came, he aimed to be ready to take advantage of it.

This day they halted at noon to eat. Though they had been riding or wallowing for hours, back and forth up the face of a vast mountainside, they had made little actual progress. The snow was too deep, the going too tough. But it was necessary to keep going, and if he could get across the mountains, Shannahan knew that his chances would be immeasureably improved.

By noon the timber was scanty. They had nearly reached timber-line. So it was doubly expedient to cook a hot meal. Shannahan had a hunch that they'd have cold food and no fire tonight, somewhere near the bleak crest of the pass.

Untying Gertney's arms, he set him to gathering wood. Melting snow for water, Shannahan mixed dough and made hot biscuits. Gertney wolfed several of them appreciatively.

"You're a better than passable cook, Shannahan," he complimented.

"We'll save the rest of the panful for supper," was Shannahan's reply. "Now your arms again."

"It's a hell of an inconvenience," Gertney complained, for the first time.

"But a great reducer of worry," Shannahan retorted, and Gertney hid a grin. If he'd get just a trifle overconfident—

In the end it was not overconfidence or lack of caution on Shannahan's part which led to Gertney's chance. They continued to climb gradually through a white world, and here the going was worse—worse because the wind had whipped much of the snow away, and the ground beneath, soaked to begin with, was now hard-frozen, icy.

Timber-line was only a quarter mile below in actual distance, more than twice that in the course they had been compelled to follow, many times as far in effort required. This looked to be the top of the pass at last, though neither man was deceived, where a man unused to mountains might have been. The steepness was less acute, and the top in reaching distance. But once attained, another and higher elevation would show ahead.

It was a respite, however, and the tired cayuses were stepping more briskly. Gertney, as always, rode ahead. His horse had no difficulty. Then, without warning, Shannahan's horse slipped on an icy patch beneath a few inches of cloaking snow. All four feet went out from under it with bewildering speed, despite its

frantic scramble to maintain itself. The next instant it had
half-slid, half-fallen for a dozen feet sideways and downslope,
to land with a thud, Shannahan caught and pinned beneath.

Gertney heard the disturbance and turned to look. He saw
how it had happened, even as he spoke an explosive Whoa to his
cayuse, realizing that here might be opportunity. Ordinarily a
rider like Shannahan would have kicked his feet loose from the
stirrups and been free before being caught, but this had
happened too fast and unexpectedly.

Gertney's horse stopped obediently at the command, and for
a moment the Acting-Secretary surveyed the situation, to
determine what he should do. Terrified, Shannahan's cayuse
strove to get on its feet again. It thrashed frantically, half raising
up, and sank back again with a heavy groan. One leg was
broken, and in that position, on such footing, it was helpless.

Much more to the point, from Gertney's point of view, was
the fact that Shannahan was pinned beneath.

Gertney had sized up the situation. But he was in no hurry. If
his hands had been free he would have moved fast. This way, he
could afford to take his time.

"You'll have to help me," Shannahan said. He had seen the
one possible chance, his eyes going to a boulder which thrust its
head above the snow, only a few feet away. Deeply embedded
in the mountain, the visible part was smooth and rounded, a few
inches wide near the top, somewhat resembling a stone hitching
post such as was in vogue before many residences in towns.

There were a lot of factors here which entered in, and some he
had to control; others he could only hope would work right. If all
did, he stood a chance. A slender one at best, since Gertney

would be aiming to turn this to his advantage. But it was this or none, and he had one hold over Gertney—the fact that his hands were still tied behind his back.

"Sure, I'll help you," Gertney agreed. The tone of his voice, more than the words, betrayed his elation. He slid to the ground, and immediately his cayuse, as if sensing how matters stood, swung around, dashed past them and vanished down the mountain at a run. With the reins looped across the saddle-horn, there was nothing to hinder it.

Gertney paused for a moment, eyeing it. He'd been afraid of that, and so had Shannahan, but there was nothing that either of them could do. There went half of their supplies, and the only remaining transportation aside from their own legs. Which could mean the difference between death or survival, high on a bleak mountain under these conditions.

Already the cayuse was disappearing in the storm. Gertney shrugged. That didn't worry him. He had a good pair of legs, and there were plenty of supplies for one man. Also it would be comparatively easy going, back down the mountain. He wouldn't have to go too far to find friends.

He advanced, and saw that Shannahan, twisting had freed one arm, and that he held something in that hand—a hunting knife which he carried in a sheath. Gertney nodded.

"That's fine," he said. "You can use it to cut me loose. And you'll do it pronto, Mister—or I'll kick your head in!"

Shannahan knew what Gertney planned, as well as if he had outlined it in detail. As soon as he was cut loose, Gertney would crush his skull with a blow of his boot, while he still lay helpless. The knife in his hand was not a weapon to fear. Or so Gertney reasoned.

Yet without Gertney's hands freed he was helpless in turn.

"Turn around," Shannahan instructed. "Scrooch down a bit."

Gertney obeyed, and felt the rope fall loose as the knife sliced through. He swung then, animosity vying with a bitter triumph in his face, and his jaw fell slack as he stared into the muzzle of Shannahan's gun.

"I knew just what you planned," Shannahan said. "But I'm still runnin' this. Lucky I could get hold of the gun as well as the knife. Now you'll do as I say or I'll kill you. Take that lariat rope and run it in a half-hitch around that rock. Tie one end to the saddle horn and bring the other back here."

Gertney obeyed in a dazed sort of manner. He had been so certain that this was his situation. But his mind quickly readjusted to the need. After all, a few minutes, or hours, didn't matter. Shannahan was hurt, very likely crippled. He in turn was free now and able-bodied. He had only to wait and watch to turn the tables.

Shannahan watched tensely while the rope was fixed. If his uneasy cayuse should start thrashing violently before preparations were complete, it could still ruin everything. Aching pain was in him, coupled with more angry stabs, the weight of the horse was agony. Like Gertney, he had no way of knowing how badly he was hurt.

He'd been lucky to a degree. The snow had made a pad which allowed him to sink into it, and took part of the strain. A hard round object which dug against his side could be nothing less than a stone, twice as big as his head. It had been concealed under the snow, but it was holding the fallen horse partially off him. Otherwise he would have been crushed.

Gertney worked efficiently, under the threat of the gun.

With the rope fastened to the saddle-horn and run around the jutting point of rock, it could give considerable leverage if the slack was properly taken up when the horse renewed its struggles. Gertney would have to attend to that.

"Hold on to your end," Shannahan instructed. "Take every bit of slack you can get—*and hold it!* Let it slip and I'll kill you, if it's the last thing I do."

"I'll do my best," Gertney agreed. He had no doubt that Shannahan would carry out his threat. It wasn't likely to work in any case, but he could afford to go along with the possibility. Before Shannahan could even stir the cayuse to action again it began to struggle violently, striving again to regain its feet. It partially succeeded, and Gertney, pulling on the rope, took up enough slack that it started to fall back, part of its weight was held.

Shannahan was already crawling back, and out. He set his teeth at the pain, fighting a wave of nausea which threatened to engulf him, but after a frantic kick his one pinioned foot came loose and he rolled aside just as the straining cayuse settled back more heavily than before, the saddle twisting with the strain.

For a moment he lay, fighting for breath, holding grimly to the gun. Gertney stared at him, a tight smile playing across his face. Then, deliberately, he turned and walked down the mountain, vanishing in the storm.

Once more the horse was trying to get to its feet, falling back, rolling its eyes. Steadying, Shannahan shot, putting an end to its agony. Grimacing, he got to his feet, and stood swaying while the mountain seemed to pitch and roll. Gradually the dizziness passed, and he was able to take stock.

No bones were broken. That could mean salvation. None, at least, in legs or arms. Internally he had not fared so well, and he guessed that several ribs were cracked or worse. It hurt to move or breathe, but he'd have to do a lot of both.

The pain slowed him considerably, just as the cold, here high on the mountain, numbed his fingers and made a fumbling process of every movement. It was a chore just to untie the rope from the saddle-horn. Now that he had it, he had to get out of the heavy overcoat, then wind the rope and around and around himself, which was a slow and clumsy job. Once it was done, it must be tightened. That would make a sheath to hold his cracked ribs in place.

Not for a moment did he dare relax his vigilance. Gertney was not such a tenderfoot as to go off down the mountain into the fast-coming night without supplies of any kind. In the constantly heavier going as the snow was thicker, wetter on the lower levels, he'd struggle only a short distance before black night overtook him, and under those conditions he'd perish. Starting off that way was a bit of deception which had not fooled Shannahan.

He had no doubt that Gertney was somewhere close, watching. So long as he kept alert and the gun handy, the Acting-Secretary wouldn't come plunging in to risk a bullet. Gertney's biggest successes had come from treachery, from outmaneuvering his opponents.

113

How long the small odds in his favor could be maintained was the question. Gertney could move ten feet to his one, and night would bring a change. It would be folly to try and trail his enemy. What he had to do was get down the mountain to timber again, where he could have a fire.

Shouldering the pack of supplies would be more than he could manage in his present condition. But it should drag down hill on the snow quite easily. Shannahan got down on his knees and started to loosen the pack, and something hurtled at him and past like a leaping ghost.

It had been a near miss—not more than three or four feet away. Shannahan moved as quickly as possible around to the opposite and lower side of the horse, and ducked down as a second missle came bounding. Now the air was full of them—a fusilade of boulders rolling down hill, dozens of them, ranging in size from a man's head to stones as big as a powerful man like Gertney could handle.

Gertney had circled, climbing up above, hidden in the storm. Looking for opportunity, he had recognized it when he came upon it in a patch of boulders high on the slope of the hill. Apparently he'd taken his time, working to gather a lot of them in one place so that he could start them with a quick grab and shove, enabling him to get many going at the same time.

All that was necessary on his part was to start them. The down slope of the mountain would do the rest. Even though a dozen or a score might miss, he figured that one ought to find its target. One would be enough. Such a leaping monster as these roaring boulders would crush a man as easily as an eggshell.

Crouching behind the inadequate shelter of the dead cayuse,

there was nothing that Shannahan could do but wait. Even if uninjured, no man could outguess a bouncing stone or outrun its wild leap. Rolling and jumping, there was no way of telling what course such a juggernaut would take on its next leap. It might continue to hurtle straight down the mountain, or, deflected, plunge crazily off at a tangent.

The air was full of them—dim-seen streaks which swooshed and whanged, a few smashing as they collided or hit other obstructions. Several struck the horse, or bounced close at hand. One passed directly over Shannahan so close that he could feel its wind. He estimated wildly that there must have been half a hundred before the torrent ceased almost as abruptly as it had begun. Gertney had run out of ammunition.

And now, of course, he'd be coming along to see what luck he'd had. Shannahan had come through the bombardment unscratched, thanks to the barrier of the horse and the slope of the hill. Gertney would be cautious enough to figure on those long odds, to take no undue chances.

But when he came, he'd aim to finish the job. If it was still to do.

The cold, now that the tenseness of flying rocks was past, made itself felt. The worrying wind nagged at flesh with bitter aggravation. Already the dead horse was stiffening, more from the chill than rigor mortis. Crouching against it no longer meant even a scanty heat transferred to his own body. Yet Shannahan dared not move until Gertney had made his play. If he could make him believe that he'd succeeded—

When finally Gertney did come he almost fooled him. The big man had circled and stalked with the feline patience of a puma. Shannahan had been watching the trail above, and he appeared from below, a big stone clutched in one fist, a club in the other. He was close, dangerously close, before Shannahan heard him.

He swung then, and Gertney hurled the stone, leaped after it with swinging club. But he too, was startled into moving too fast. The stone missed, as had its more ponderous predecessors. Shannahan fired.

His intention had been to put lead through Gertney's arm, which cluched the club. He had no desire to kill, not at this stage of the game. In any case, Gertney was important alive—vital almost, to his own hope of ever coming out of these hills.

But again the need for too much haste spoiled things. With the big man plunging uphill and the storm still playing tricks with vision, it was hard to estimate, impossible for a careful aim. Gertney went down, sprawling. Blood made a spilling strain across the snow.

For a moment, as badly frightened as hurt, Gertney bawled like a calf. He bellowed in frenzy and struggled to sit up, and flopped back. Then he quieted, and sat staring at his own left leg, a useless thing as it stretched before him.

Dismay coursed in Shannahan in almost equal measure. Better to have killed the man, he thought, than this. The spirit and the fight had all gone out of Gertney. He turned his head and fear was in his eyes.

"Now we're finished," he said. "Both of us."

"Maybe not," Shannahan contradicted, and crawled toward him. The bullet had plowed its course not far above the knee on the fleshy part of the leg. Going in and out again, a nasty wound. But apparently it had broken no bones.

Which, under these conditions, made little difference. It would be impossible for Gertney to walk.

"There's one sure thing," Shannahan said sharply. "The only chance that either one of us has is if we both work together. I'll do my best for you if you'll do the same for me. Do I have your word to play square till we're out of the woods?"

Fear and terror had mastered Gertney moments before. Which was hardly to be wondered at, high on a bleak mountain with a dirge in the wind. Now, under the stimulus of Shannahan's example, something of the spirit which had made him so formidable returned. Gertney nodded.

"That's sense," he admitted. "You've my word—if it helps any."

"The first thing is to stop that bleeding," Shannahan said matter-of-factly, and unloosened the neckerchief from about his own throat. It made a passable bandage, tied tightly, and the bleeding was mostly checked. The application of cold snow aided. By now, however, the shock was beginning to take effect on both men, the real pain to tear at them.

"We've got to get down to timber," Shannahan said grimly. "Without a fire tonight we're finished."

He loosened the pack which had been tied behind the saddle, an operation delayed by the hurtling boulders. Partly opening the pack, he spread out the blanket beside Gertney.

"Slide on," he instructed. "I'll try and drag you along. It's down hill, which helps."

117

Gertney looked up, aroused out of a half-coma of pain. His face was dull with hopelessness, but he slid and wriggled on to the spread-out pack and blanket. The impossibility of the thing was in his eyes.

"You can't make it, Shannahan," he protested. "If you weren't banged up it would be bad enough. This way we're finished, and we might as well admit it."

"Men have done the impossible plenty of times, because they had to," Shannahan reminded him. "If I can't pull you, you'll crawl!"

And that, in the long run, was what he forced Gertney to do. For the first hundred yards down-slope, where the going was fairly smooth and even, the snow not too deep he managed to drag the pack with Gertney's weight upon it. Pain pushed at him so that the breath squeezed out of his lungs, but he tugged and moved.

Then, where the snow lay deeper, the going rougher, it was out of the question. The pack simply bogged down and stuck.

"I'll drag it and make trail," Shannahan said. "You'll crawl and drag your leg."

He managed the pack with the added weight removed, but Gertney, the little reserve of courage already run out of him, whimpered and quit.

"I can't," he protested. "It's killing me."

"You'll crawl," Shannahan told him, and dragged the gun into his hand again "Crawl, damn you—or I'll kill you!"

Somehow, alternately threatening and cajoling, he got him down to timber-line. Already the dark was settling, though the white snow gave a last thin measure of light. In it, Shannahan found what he had noticed on the way up—a twisted, snow-smothered mass which proved to be a windfall.

It was a tortured pile upon the side of the mountain. Here, braving the elements which had decreed that this was the final limit where life might survive during the long months when the arctic made rendezvous upon the hills, a clump of trees had taken root and prospered in defiance of the edict. Partial shelter had been afforded them by an outcrop of the sheltering ledge above. They had attained a better size than any others so high on the mountain.

As if watching this effort and waiting only the proper time, the storm gods had had their way. Now all that remained was a wind-fall, a twisted and broken mass of wreckage nearly hidden by the snow.

It took time and effort to work a way in and among this pile, but Shannahan managed. Back in there, as he had known would be the case, was wood in plenty, broken some of it dry despite the storm. He got a fire going, and in its warmth was survival.

By the light of the fire he cooked a good meal. The sickness of pain was in both of them, but hunger was stronger. Cold and the drag of bitter exertion demanded food. They ate heartily, and felt better for it. And then they shared the remaining blanket together.

Something roused Shannahan during the night, but it was too dark to see, too difficult to move. On the verge of complete exhaustion, he had slept heavily, as though drugged, and Gertney was doing the same.

Whatever it was, he heard no more, and dropped off to sleep again. Daylight found him cold and stiff, aching in every joint.

The clouds were breaking, the long storm finally at an end. Here on the mountain he judged that it must be zero at least, and the wind, busy as always, added to the sting.

The fire, smouldering among some of the tumbled pile of logs, had long since gone out. Shannahan found some smaller, dry wood and got a new fire going. Not until that did the lethargy of pain and cold lift enough that he thought to look around. Then he saw what had disturbed him during the night.

A prowling bear—and an enormous one, by the looks of the prints in the snow—had visited them, attracted by the odor of food in the pack. Finding that a little way off, it had been content. But what it had not eaten it had ruined. Save for the blankets under which they had slept, the gun and the matches in his pocket, their supplies were gone.

MORGAN REARDON was a western senator in more than name. He had been born in a covered wagon and raised on the trail. All his life had been a fight, first for survival, then for what he wanted or believed in. Always he had been a man of action, and several years of wearing the figurative toga had not changed that.

He had enlisted in this struggle to save the reservation whole-heartedly. Sam Shannahan was his friend, as Shannahan's father had been. That in itself would have been enough, for Reardon never forgot a friend, just as, in his own uncompromising code, he never forgave an enemy.

This matter of the Indian lands, all too despoiled in contravention of treaties, was close to the Senator's heart. To him it

120

was not alone a matter of justice for the Indians, but a matter of honor for his country, which he helped represent. Treaties, in his estimation, should be as binding as a man's word. Beyond that no honest man could go.

The delays of train travel irked him, as they always did. Better a good horse between his legs than a jouncing car and the stench of coal smoke drifting back. The trouble was that, when he traveled, the Senator was always in a hurry. This time his impatience burned more brightly than usual.

The swirling drive of rain, blanking away the country-side, dimming the towns they passed through, added to his fuming desire for speed, but brought delays. A glance down as they rumbled across bridges shoed streams swollen and angry. And finally, just as he had begun to count the remaining miles, the train stopped completely, with the news that the roadway had been washed out.

Fortunately they were not too far from a town. Reasonably good accommodations could be obtained there, the conductor gave assurance, until such time as the journey could be resumed.

"And when will that be?" Reardon roared. "Hang it, I'm in a hurry!"

The conductor was apologetic.

"I'm awfully sorry, Senator. But it will be a matter of days—three or four, at the very least. There's a bridge gone, and a section of the right of way. Two or three hundred yards in all. But you'll be comfortable in town—"

"I wouldn't be comfortable a minute, waiting there when

I've got to get to Antelope," Reardon denied. "But I'm not blaming the railroad for this. I suppose the stage is still running?"

"I doubt it,sir. I understand that the highway bridge has been washed out as well, and the creek—well, you can see for yourself, sir. It's a regular river."

"Rivers can be swum," said the Senator tersely. "Let's get back to town. I'll find out."

As predicted, the stage was not running. Old Lige Crabshaw, who had tooled it over virtually impossible roads for a decade, had been willing to risk hell or high water if his passengers felt the same way about it.

But, reaching the creek, beholding its untamed sweep, with uprooted trees jiggled on its crest and other debris swept along at its whim, they had sat and watched and felt their courage drain out. Lige had still expressed a willingness to make the venture if they gave the go-ahead. None had given it.

This news made a clamor in the Senator's ears.

"It would be suicide to try, suh. That creek's usually fifty feet across. Now it's three hundred yards, and no bridge. No bottom either. It couldn't be done."

"It's got to be done," Reardon snapped. "I've swum trail herds across the Red, the Canadian and the Blue when they were flooded, and if anybody thinks those streams are a picnic, I'd suggest he try it. How about it, Lige? You takin' me to Antelope?"

Crabshaw combed lean fingers through a sparse fringe of whitening beard and nodded.

"Hell, yes," he agreed. "If'n we get drowned, it won't be

the first time, eh? Somebody tell the boys to hook up the team. I got to get me a couple of quick ones first."

He had taken them straight by the time the stage rolled up, hoofs squelching in the mud, the steel tires cutting thin ribbons through it. Half-drunk now, his blood warmed, Lige was ready for what might lie ahead, but by way of precaution he stuffed a fresh flask into his coat pocket.

"You want to ride inside, Senator, or on the box with me?" he inquired. "Dryer, inside, mebby, but easier to swim from outside."

"I can't swim a lick, but I'd be soaked, anyway, 'fore we crossed the creek," Reardon grunted, and climbed over the wheel and up beside him. "Let's roll."

They came within sight of the flood, and Crabshaw, driving with one hand, reached for his flask. He extracted the cork with his teeth, and drank, not slowing the horses, head tipped back into the beat of the rain. He gauged the amount closely, tendered what remained to the Senator.

"Kill 'er, Morg," he said. You'll need 'er!"

Reardon obeyed, noting that now Lige Crabshaw was - swinging his long whip and shouting, putting the horses to a dead run as they neared the creek. He was giving them no chance to hesitate, and, equally important, no chance for hesitation in himself.

"The longer you look at somethin' like that, the worse it gets," he grunted. "Tried it one time, and scared a year's growth out of myself. Been two inches shorter ever since. So I shore as hell ain't stoppin' to study the beauties none!"

Now the horses were in, splashing, swimming all at once.

The stage swayed, jolted, lifted to the current, dragged, and whipped downstream while the six horses swam desperately and were pulled with it. A hugh log swept out of the rainy mist and surged at them, then plowed sullenly by, inches behind. The stage rolled and pitched in imminent danger of overturning, but Lige's hand was steady on the reins, his voice encouraging, his eyes calculating. All at once the horses found footing, scrambled, and the wheels jerked on rocks.

They emerged, dripping, nearly half a mile downstream from where they had entered on the opposite bank, far below the road. But Lige, grinning briefly, found a trail and worked back to the ribbon of mud.

"Them other fellers missed a ride," he commented. "Still, I guess it's just as well. Too much extry weight wouldn't a helped none."

"I'm going to send you a new outfit, Lige, from boots to hat, once I get back to Washington," the Senator said appreciatively.

"Thankee, Morg. My best is gettin' kinda frowsty."

Progress was slow. The mud was deep, the road washed badly in places, or deep in debris shoved down by wild water. The rain still pelted without let-up. Beside the road, where for a change it ran almost straight, was the line of poles and the strung dark wire of the telegraph. A wire which, not much farther on, dangled helplessly between two of the poles.

Reardon frowned at it, his glance calculating. They made another quarter of a mile, and pulled up as two men stepped into the road with rifles crooked carelessly in their arms.

"You can't go any farther," one of the gunmen stated. "Washout ahead."

"Take more'n a washout to stop me," Crabshaw said, but warily. "I been over bad roads before—or the places where they was."

"Then, if it'll more to ding sense into that thick head of yore's, take a look at these guns," the speaker suggested softly. "What I mean is, you've gone far enough."

Lige Crabshaw had both hands full with the reins. Whatever needed to be done was up to the Senator. Which was well enough with both of them, for he was adequate to the occasion. The men in the road had plainly been surprised at sight of them, though posted here to take no chances. But they were too confident of themselves, their guns held carelessly. They stiffened in amazement at sight of the big revolver which seemed to jump into Reardon's hand, its muzzle cannon-like.

But they were men who took their job seriously. The one who had said nothing tried to bring his weapon to bear in a quick sweep, and Crabshaw saw that it was not a rifle, but a shotgun. One quick blast would be enough, without the need of aim.

The guard's trouble was to get his gun up. Reardon's woke the echoes, and the shotgun dropped in the mud, its late owner flopping face down across it. An instant later Reardon was off the stage and alongside the other outlaw. With calculated deliberateness, even as the rifle dropped and hands jerked skyward, he clipped the man alongside the head with the barrel of his revolver.

It was a smart blow, not too hard. A clout which drew blood

and rocked the bandit on his feet. It sent sick fear into his eyes, but he steadied and saved himself from falling.

"Who sent you fellows out in all this rain to stop us?" the Senator demanded. "Talk fast!"

Only for an instant did the gunman hesitate. At the implacable will in Reardon's eyes he answered.

"It was Rees Hosty. He sent us."

"Who is he?"

"He owns the Powder Horn Saloon in Antelope."

"Ah!" Understanding came to the Senator's eyes. "Gertney's man, eh?"

"Yeah, I reckon so."

"That's fine. And I'm Senator Reardon. Your job was to stop me. Right?"

"Yeah, that's it. I—we didn't mean—"

"I know what you mean. Now I want to know some other things. Don't keep me waiting."

During the next few minutes Reardon extracted sufficient information to bring him up to date on events at Antelope, at least so far as this man was informed. He'd left town the day before, and that time lapse must be taken into consideration.

But it all sounded bad enough. Worse, in some respects, than Reardon had anticipated. He turned impatiently to Crabshaw, ignoring the dead man.

"Take this fellow's gun and keep him from runnin' away," he instructed. "They've cut the telegraph, back a way. I'll go fix it and have a talk with Washington. With the President, I think. Then we'll go on."

Lige Crabshaw nodded, unsurprised. It was no news to him

126

that a United States Senator, at least this particular one, intended to climb a pole and fix a broken wire, or send a message when he got to the top. Lige remembered when Morg Reardon had worked with the company, helping set poles and string wires for this first spanning of the continent with the talking wire. That hadn't been so long ago—just shortly before he'd gone back to Washington as a Senator.

Reardon was heavier now, but he could do the job. Including tapping out a message, providing the line was intact from the break on east.

That it might not be was a gamble, but one important enough to take. He'd need tools, wire to splice the cut.

"Reckon I'll have to take your buggy apart, Lige," he apologized, and untwisted a length of bailing wire which had been used to repair a break in the luggage railing which ran around the top of the stage.

Next he lifted the hub wrench which also held the whiffletrees in place. With this equipment he splashed through the mud, back along the road, finding it considerably more of an effort than he anticipated.

"Getting soft!" he grunted. "Too much Washington! I'd ought to have climbers, too—but I guess I can manage! Not as tough as knockin' out a message from a caboose with Indians howlin' outside and firing through."

Reaching the break, he climbed laboriously to the top of a post, where the wire had first been cut, as the neat slice proved. He was about to make his test when a voice spoke from below.

"Get down from there—and pronto! Or do I have to shoot you down?"

127

The Senator turned slowly, gazing down. On the ground at the foot of the pole were two more men, apparently companions of the pair who had stopped the stage, whom the other man had carefully neglected to mention. They had slipped out of a nearby patch of trees and brush, and gave every appearance of meaning business. Looking down into the muzzle of the gun uptilted his way, Reardon knew just how big his own must have looked in the reverse case.

Chapter Seven

YESTERDAY THE mountains had been sheathed in storm. Today they were a white wilderness. the sun was back in the sky, but in the few days since first the rain had come it had retreated to a remote entity, its summer warmth gone, seeming to retain only brightness.

That quality was torment to the eyes, relieved partially by the evergreens where the snow had shaken loose. Now they had reached the belt of trees again, and these afforded rest as well as shelter. Shannahan preferred to move among them, to keep screened from the observation of any sharp eyes in the valley below, or where men might prowl the hills. Gertney was aghast at this decision.

"But the only chance that we have is to be seen, to get help as soon as we can," he protested. "Get me back, and I won't prefer any charges against you, Shannahan. But if we try to hide out up here, we'll die."

"We may," Shannahan agreed. "That's a chance we're

taking. I set out to remove you from the scene until such time as you can do no more damage. And you'll stay away till then, if it kills both of us.''

Gertney's earlier calm was shattered. He protested, pleading, promising to do anything, to refrain from any action, if only they could get back to help. Shannahan heard him, unmoved.

''We won't starve—or freeze, not yet a while,'' he said. ''I've matches for a fire, and I can kill game, and cook it. As for your promises, Gertney, you wouldn't keep them a split second longer than it seemed profitable. You know it and I know it, and so you'll just have to suffer for your reputation.''

Finding argument useless, Gertney grew sullen. He was getting soft, he admitted to himself. These latter years of good living, years spent in a swivel chair instead of out on the trail, had taken a lot out of him. Hardship struck now like a taloned hawk into the soft flesh of its victim.

His predicament was desperate. Machinery had been set in motion, back in Washington. Usually, like the mills of the gods, that machinery ground at a snail's pace, but sooner or later, inevitably, it would catch up with him, the situation would get out of control. Regardless of what happened there, the swarm of homeseekers would not wait forever. You had to pick a melon when it was ripe, or have it spoil on your hands. This scheme was that sort of a melon.

Thought of the fortune which had been all but within his grasp enraged him. He refused sullenly to cooperate in any respect.

''If I've got to die out here anyway. I'll do nothing to keep you alive,'' he growled. ''You're being a fool, Shannahan. Is it a cut you want? If it is, say so. On my word of honor, I'll give

130

you half—enough to make you independent for life.''

"You usually win by bribery, don't you?'' Shannahan asked.

"I've never found a man yet that didn't have his price. I've been a fool not to think what you were really driving at. Naturally, you are in it for what you can get. You're a white man, the same as I am. So why should you have any love for the Indians?''

"The best answer that I can think of, to that, is your claim to being a white man,'' Shannahan answered, and saw the naked hate which looked out of Gertney's eyes.

Three or four times, that day, they saw searchers, scouring the country outspread below. So long as they remained this high, among the trees, there was no trail for their pursuers. The continuing storm and the ever-busy wind had taken care of that. Not once, that day, did any come close enough to be a menace. And the many trails which the searchers were making, in their work, would only add confusion.

Game trails were also appearing, here among the trees where the wind quested in vain. Rabbit tracks made a profusion. Mice, weasels and then, in swift rising crescendo, up to larger game—the prowl of a fisher cat, the great pads of a lynx. Coyote and their larger cousins, the wolves. The track of a bear, moving urgently, his nerves twanging with the knowledge that it was time to be denning up for the winter.

They were beyond the reservation's edge, though not far. Back in the mountains for which Shannahan had headed, knowing that only among them would he find sanctuary. His hope to cross to the far side had not been realized, but the storm had helped, even though in other ways it had been a hinderance.

By tomorrow the situation would be worse. He had no doubt that the searchers would have found the pony which Gertney had ridden, and would be sure from that that those they sought had not crossed the barrier. Having pretty well scoured the lower, more accessible country today, they would presently be forced to the more arduous task of coming higher.

Once their trail was found, it would be ticklish. It was a situation to which Shannahan could think of no solution. They could not move fast or far, or hide their trail.

"You'd better hope that they don't find us," he again warned his morose captive. "If they do, that will be just too bad for you."

Gertney was uncomfortably sure that he meant it. He'd tried more than once, personally and through agents, to kill Shannahan. The charges against Shannahan, if he was taken now, and particularly with Gertney alive to press them, were such that he'd be no worse off for killing him in turn. Though Gertney knew well enough that it was not such thoughts which motivated this strange, recklessly wild Irishman. He'd set out to save the reservation, and he'd go to any limit to do it. That was a strange philosophy, one beyond Gertney's understanding. But he knew that it was so.

His leg pained him considerably, though the wound had been a clean one and was doing well, despite its lack of care. Gertney had some fever as the day wore on, but not too much. Mostly it helped to warm him against the continuing chill at this altitude. Up here, where the sun hardly penetrated through the trees, it was winter, even though some of the snow might be softening in

132

the valleys, might even be giving way to patches of bare ground at Antelope.

Shannahan found himself better than he'd dared hope, though it hurt to breathe and to move. But not too much. He was bruised and sore, and those cracked ribs—he'd about decided that maybe they were not broken—were doing as well as could be expected. They were no longer a serious source of worry.

Nor did the future worry him—not if he could keep Gertney out here long enough. Once the Secretary returned, and Senator Reardon could bring his influence to bear, Gertney would not only have failed, but he would be forced to resign, badly discredited. Shannahan might face a jail term, but with Reardon defending him, he was as apt to be hailed as a hero.

None of which worried him particularly. What concerned him now was to do this job. He'd started it, and he wanted to finish it.

Late that afternoon he knocked over a rabbit with a stick. It was not too difficult, biding his time along a runway. They ate well of roast rabbit, building a fire in a sheltered spot after dark.

Before real daylight he repeated the ruse with a flung stick at a grouse.

But today, as he watched the movement of the searchers, he saw that they were going to do what he had expected—scour the higher country. That was difficult and tedious, with a vast amount of rough land to be covered. But there were a lot of men spread on the search, and it would take luck to evade them. Skill might have availed, but he would have no chance to use it.

Gertney was less feverish. His mind was clear, so that he

knew what was going on. His hope was strong that they would be found. He didn't believe that Shannahan would kill him with others coming at them. That would be murder, and he'd hang for it.

As if reading his thoughts. Shannahan turned to look at him.

"If they were hot on our trail, sure of us, I *might* bargain," he said, and Gertney knew that he would have points about which to argue. "But if they're just searching, and you try and attract their attention—it'll be just too bad!"

There was a change in the air today. The sun seemed less bright, more remote. Haze was beginning to fill the valleys. Another storm was on the way. Which was nothing unusual for the season of year at this high altitude. The prospect filled Gertney with fresh terror.

Now there was nothing to do but wait. Shannahan had chosen a good position. They were well sheltered, yet from their covert it was possible to observe widely. Noon came and went, and the air was growing colder, the sun getting more remote as the haze continued to spread.

All at once, three men, soldiers, came into sight. Both men watched intently, and Shannahan moved closer to Gertney, picking up the revolver which had lain in his lap. He drew back the trigger with ominous warning, and held the muzzle inches from Gertney's head. He did not voice a threat, and the lack of that was doubly convincing.

It was soon clear that the three who had come this high had done so on speculation, without discovering any trail. They came on, taking a course which must bring them straight to the covert if they held to it. Then they swerved starting down the hill

134

again. There was a sergeant and two privates. They paused while the officer stuffed a stubby pipe and got it alight.

"We'd best be getting back," he said. "We've found nothing, and it's my opinion that there's nothing to find, this side of the divide. There'll be more storm tonight. Which means that nobody will cross back or forth again till spring."

"What you're sayin' then, Sergeant, is that this finishes the search?"

"I didn't say that. But it's my opinion it does, at least for this section of country. We've combed it thoroughly and found nothing."

They moved down hill faster. Gertney half raised up, his mouth opening. Then he felt the cold steel rimming his bare flesh at the neck, and sank back. Unreasoning terror was in his eyes.

"They're gone!" he choked. "Gone, and with them the last hope we had! A new storm, and us not able to travel! Now we'll *both* die, you fool!"

"SO YOU want me to come down, is that it?" Senator Reardon gazed at the pair on the ground below, one standing almost at the foot of the pole, holding the gun, the other back a few feet. A more unprepossessing pair, he decided, he'd never seen.

"You've got the idea, feller," the gunman agreed. "Come down here, and quick about it! And if you reach for that gun, you'll come down a damn sight faster than you went up!"

"I'll do that anyway," Reardon grunted, and let go. It was fifteen feet down, and with the weight he had been putting on of

135

late years he could easily break a leg. Not his own, he hoped, and landed spread-eagled on top of the man at the foot of the pole, who had tried, too late, to jump back.

They went to the ground together, and Reardon came to his feet again with a speed which would not have surprised those that had known him of old. A glance assured him that the man who had broken his tumble would give no trouble for a while. He seemed peacefully asleep.

It was almost too easy. Reardon's blood had been sluggish of late, and he was getting a pleasureable thrill out of this renewal of his youth. But the gun which he now had in his hand took all the fight out of the second man.

"I didn't come here to get killed," the outlaw protested. "That wan't in the bargain at all."

"You're a sensible man—and sensible men are the curse of our country," the Senator assured him glumly. "Only the adventurous ever bring about any change or progress. Just in case your friend should wake up with a grouch, you'd better tie him up. You can use that rope you brought along."

He suspected that the rope might have been intended for a similar use on himself, but the job was done with a pleasing zeal. Using what remained of the rope, he made the second man fast. Then, freed of interruption, he resumed the task at the top of the pole.

His instruments were crude. But he had used even less efficient tools before in time of crisis, and had been commended as an excellent telegrapher under difficulties.

Now, finding the line in working order, he tapped out an indignant message to the President, knowing that, with the

136

details of these latest outrages for a spur, he would get some action.

"Which won't do any good unless Shannahan has managed to keep the situation under control, up to now," he sighed. "And if he's in jail, no telling what I'll find when I get there."

In turn, he got in touch with Antelope, enough to be assured that the wire was now intact in both directions. Coming down, this time more slowly, he saw that the first man had regained consciousness. Cutting loose his now subdued prisoners, he trudged back to the stage, to find Crabshaw keeping stern watch over his own.

"Let him go, too," Reardon ordered. "I think he's had enough. I know I have," he added, as he climbed wearily to the box again, having returned the whiffletree bolt to its place. "I guess I must be getting old, Lige. I can't think of anything that would look half so good to me, right now, as bed."

"Tain't mor'n another thutty miles over these washed-out roads," Crabshaw explained comfortingly. "We'll make it there by'midnight, with good luck."

They rolled in to town, half an hour short of that deadline, and the senator aroused sufficiently to learn that Shannahan had not only escaped, but had kidnapped Gertney and taken him back into the hills.

"So I might just as well have stayed in Washington, except for the fun of the thing," he sighed. "And I wouldn't have missed that for anything. Though I wouldn't do it again for a million dollars!"

It was not a pretty story which Dot Hauswirth had to tell, once the effects of the drug had worn off. Her own feelings had been confused, torn between loyalty to her father and doubt as to how much he had been prejudiced against a man who really wanted to make restitution. All doubt was gone now, and Mike McLeod, hearing the story, was torn between rage and despair.

"There's one sure thing," he said, with a boldness which astonished himself. "You're not going to marry Gertney, now or ever. When you marry anybody, it's going to be me!"

"I wouldn't have married him anyway," Dorothy confessed. Then, coloring rosily, she retreated hastily into another room.

Out of this emerged one certainty for the Major. He'd have to keep on hunting Shannahan and Gertney. Though with the passing of time he was becoming doubtful of what he might find, if anything. The mountains had a way of clutching secrets to themselves, of holding on to them.

The arrival of Senator Reardon was a spur. By morning, when he had rested from his trip, he was busy again, sending messages to Washington, conferring with McLeod. But having done all that he could, he confessed to a fit of despondency.

"Gertney's a scoundrel. Not a doubt of that, to my mind. He's one of the political mistakes that sometimes occur, just as such men manage to worm their way into positions of trust in industry, with the purpose of picking the bones for themselves. The trouble is, while we know all that, there's nothing much that we can do.

"I've placed the facts before the President—such facts as I have. They're shocking enough, but nothing to justify him in taking action over the head of his Secretary of the Interior, who is still in Europe. And the Atlantic Cable is still broken."

He jumped to his feet, paced irritably back and forth, then sat down again.

"Those hoodlums who tried to stop me from getting here—there's no doubt in my mind that they were working for Gertney. But he was smart enough to have underlings send them on the job, and the only name I got from them was that of Goodman. Apparently he's a killer and a wanted man, but you say that Gertney has vigorously condemned him in public! He would, of course—he's shrewd. So where does that leave us? Nowhere, until the Secretary returns, or Shannahan gets back. He seems to be keeping Gertney out of the way, but I don't like the situation too well, for all that."

"There's one man who might be able to tell us something, if we could find him," McLeod said slowly. "That's Bob LaFontise. The trouble is, he seems to have disappeared as completely as Shannahan. I have a notion that he's helping him."

In that guess, McLeod was accurate enough, through not as concerned the method. LaFontise had made no effort to join his friend. Having devoted some thought to the subject, it had occurred to him that the simplest way to find where Sid McLeod was being held captive was to ask those who were holding him. That would have to be done deviously and by indirection, but LaFontise had considerable skill at that.

He gauged correctly that Nick Duffy and Rees Hosty would be the men most likely to possess the information. Hosty would hardly do to approach. He might remember LaFontise's vigorous protest against his diatribe concerning reservation lands.

But Nick Duffy should be a good man to work with.

The first necessity was whiskey, and, to have any effect on the Agent, it must be whiskey of high potency. He was so soaked in ordinary liquor that he could absorb it like a sponge, and with less apparent effect. But some of the whiskey that Rees Hosty sold illegally to the Indians—trade or Indian whiskey—that, if Duffy could be induced to drink it, should get results. Old timers, knowing its potency, graphically called it rattlesnake juice.

The preliminaries were not difficult. A friend gave proper directions, and LaFontise, appearing as a white man, explained that he wanted some of it for certain Indian friends with whom he had business to transact. Hosty's bar-tender had no scruples nor orders to the contrary when the proper price was put in his hand. He furnished the liquor, adding a word of warning.

"That stuff's all right for an Injun," he cautioned. "But don't make the mistake of tryin' none yoreself, even to see what a cast-iron stummick can handle. That mixture's mostly raw alcohol, soap an' terbacker an' a strong footin' of arsenic to give it a kick. An' believe me, mister, it'd kill anything less'n an Injun. Kills some of them now an' then, but nobody cares about that. The doc, when he finds such a case, he just puts it down as snake bite."

LaFontise accepted the whiskey and the advice with proper appreciation.

"I want a quart of your very best whiskey for myself," he added. "Not the sort you serve your customers, either. The kind that gentlemen drink."

A bottle was given him, plentifully sealed with gold foil.

140

"You can't go wrong with this," he was assured. "It's the sort that Mr. Gertney and Hosty both drink. Mr. Duffy, too—though between you and me, he wouldn't know the difference it it wasn't for the label."

That was as LaFontise had guessed. He worked carefully for a while, opening the bottles and transferring the contents, discarding the good whiskey and substituting tea in the unlabeled bottle. The gold foil looked unblemished when he had finished. With this product, he sought out the Agent.

"What I'm really here for," he confided to Nick Duffy, having given his own name as Smith, "is to secure some private information pertaining to conditions in this country. It requires a particularly well-informed man to furnish that, and after careful inquiry, I'm convinced that you're the one man who can give it to me. And just to make it a social occasion, I've brought along a bottle."

There was no difficulty. Nick Duffy conceded that he was unquestionably the man to come to for information. Within a couple of hours he was sufficiently dazed with the rattlesnake juice to be led, by devious paths, to the information which LaFontise really desired. He had started a little at the first taste of the whiskey, turning for a surprised stare at the label. Reassured by the visual evidence, he declared that it seemed better than usual, and poured himself a second drink. Now, thoroughly mellowed, he pounded the table with his fist.

"Ish all in knowin' how, managin' people. Yesshir! Major might a been difficult. But with his brother for a hos-hoshtage—why, no trouble 'tall! Notabit!"

One more drink and LaFontise had the location where the

hostage was being held. It was a remote cabin, back in a gorge in the hills, some three miles from town. Having left the Agent deep in a drunken sleep, he approached the cabin cautiously but without challenge. Reaching the door, he threw it open suddenly, gun in hand.

The precautions were scarcely necessary. There were three men in the room, seated on the floor, playing dice in desultory fashion. Sid McLeod and his guards.

"I'm mighty glad to see you," Sid declared, as soon as they had the situation to LaFontise's liking, the other two tied fast to chairs. "There hasn't been a thing to do to kill time but roll the bones, and as usual, I've had the devil's own luck. I always seem to lose."

LaFontise stooped and scooped up the scattered dice. He fingered them, threw them speculatively a couple of times.

"Before you gamble any more, Sid," he suggested. "You should learn the fundamentals. No wonder your luck is always bad. You company with professionals, but you're worse than a sheep among wolves. You're a fool among crooks. These are loaded. You should have known. You had no gambler's debt to Rees Hosty. You can tell him so, in your brother's presence —that you were merely being played for a sucker."

Sid swore for a minute and then looked up at Bob sheepishly. "I guess I am a fool, letting those crooks take me in like that. Maybe I deserved it, but I'm sorry for Mike now. He's always had to pay for my mistakes." He remained silent for a minute, then continued in a firm voice, "Look, Bob, I'm not going back with you. I'll strike out across the hills and make for some other

142

part of the country. You tell Mike what happened and if he ever hears from me again, it won't be because I'm in trouble."

REES HOSTY had been badly frightened. It had seemed to him that his world was slipping like shale rock from beneath his feet, leaving nothing at which to grab. The cool nerve of Shannahan in using him for an instrument, then kidnapping Gertney from under the very noses of his friends, had been something considerably beyond the saloon keeper's experience.

Reflection and time, however, had made a difference. Once he had recovered from the effect of that gun-barrel alongside his head, he could plan as craftily as before, and now he was in a mood to believe Nick Duffy, that something might be salvaged. The army, under McLeod, was running around in circles. Even the arrival of Senator Reardon had not changed things.

The simple truth was that power still lay in the hands of Gertney, if he could exercise it. Until such time as his superior returned from Europe, he could act—if given a chance. No amount of sound or fury on the part of others could change that, nor threats of what they would do later. Threats, Hosty knew, would move Gertney not at all.

The only real impediment was Shannahan. And he was no light stumbling-block. But when the searchers returned with word that one of the horses, presumably the one ridden by Gertney, had come in, reins still looped across the saddle-horn, Hosty took new hope.

Something had gone wrong, on this side of the mountains. Something, it was easy to guess, in which Gertney had had a

143

hand. Knowing the Acting-Secretary, Hosty felt new confidence. Gertney would be back, sooner or later. He was that kind of a man.

The job now—Hosty's own—was to have things under control when Gertney returned. If that was done, they'd still be an unbeatable combination.

The Major had been spurred to greater action by finding the horse, despatching every available man on a fresh hunt. Hosty was under no delusions concerning McLeod. Ostensibly he was cooperating with him, but that was a sort of help on which the saloon keeper placed no dependence. But that didn't matter. He had made up his mind that Gertney would be coming back.

That faith, that the Acting-Secretary would be in command of the situation, was severely shaken during the early afternoon. Hosty climbed to the roof of his saloon, which he had long since discovered to be an excellent observation post. A careful look toward the hills showing him two men, still a couple of miles away, making a painful way toward town.

Hosty was sharp-eyed. Now, not trusting to his own, he hurried down to his office. Returning presently with a pair of field-glasses, he brought the pigmy-like figures into focus and watched tensely.

It was as he had suspected—these were Shannahan and Gertney. The trouble was that Shannahan appeared to be in control.

If it could be called by such a term. He plodded in the snow, or rather staggered, tugging at a rope. This in turn was attached to a crude sort of sled made of saplings, and on it sprawled the inert mass of Nillo Gertney. Apparently he was too sick or badly injured to help himself. Shannahan, though he was pulling the sled, appeared in little better shape.

The field glasses brought them into sharp relief, showing the ravages of the past several days—cold, hunger, lack of food and sleep, fever and injury. Both men looked to be in the last stages of exhaustion. Shannahan toiled stubbornly, with a dogged persistence, not only to reach town himself, but to bring Gertney along.

Twice, while Hosty watched, Shannahan stumbled and fell in the snow. Each time he got up again, with a courage which bordered on the pathetic.

"If he ain't so dangerous to us, I'd come mighty close to admirin' him," Hosty grunted to himself. "Reckon he figgers one of two things. Either than he can control things, once he gets back. Or else Gertney's had enough, and has busted down and promised to do anything, just to save his own neck. It could be both."

Hosty's guess was shrewd. Gertney had indeed broken down, as completely as a man may go to pieces. He was sick with fever, racked with pain, for the constant movement was hard on his injured leg. For all that, it was doing well enough, healing without any sign of infection. But Gertney, believing that it was getting steadily worse, convinced that he would be bait for wolves if they stayed out much longer, had raved and pleaded and taken the most solemn oaths of which his tormented mind could conceive, in an effort to get Shannahan to return.

On Shannahan's part there was not much choice. The long strain was telling on him, getting worse with every hour. Gertney had been able to help himself at first. Now everything

145

devolved on Shannahan. He knew that he had to get back. And he still hoped that time and events would have taken a hand.

The simplest way would have been to leave Gertney. That was what the Secretary would have done in similar case, as his fears and impassioned pleas not to desert him proved. But Shannahan had no intention of leaving him. He'd taken him out, and he'd bring him back.

Hosty, having studied the situation, was ready to act. Either by luck or skill, Shannahan had made it this far without being found by the searchers. If he could get a little farther he'd be among friends, and in control.

But if he didn't reach friends—! Not only was most of the army out in a vast new hunt for these men, but McLeod headed the search, accompanied by the Senator. The fact that the army was off in the hills could make all the difference—the margin by which victory might still be snatched.

Hosty was smiling confidently as he hurried to the street. There were only a handful of men left at the post. But here in town were dozens of hangers-on whom he could trust. And, among the land-seekers who had been milling in ever increasing discontent for the last few days, there were hundreds —thousands. Give them leadership, the promise of the land which up to now they had been denied and he'd have an overwhelming force behind him.

Issuing swift orders, Hosty started on a run for the livery stable. He intended to get a horse and personally direct operations. Then, as he neared it, he was accosted by a man who blocked his path.

"I'm in a hurry now," Hosty panted. "See you later—"

Then, recognizing Jinks Gordy, he stopped.

"You got somethin' new from Washington?" he demanded.

Gordy nodded, smiling crookedly.

"I sure have," he agreed. "It just come in. Two messages—three when it comes to that. One for Senator Reardon, one for Shannahan. And one for Gertney, ef'n he shows up to get it."

Hosty promptly drew his emmisary into the livery stable, back into the seclusion of a stall.

"Did you take them, or the agent?" he demanded.

"He did. But I found out what come in, same as you said to do. And then I didn't waste no time gettin' to you. It seems that the Atlantic cable has been fixed. The President himself has talked to the Secretary, over in Europe, and got action. That's Reardon's doing, of course."

"Never mind that," Hosty jerked out impatiently. "What are those messages?"

"Orders to Gertney not to take any action about the reservation, not till his boss has got back and had a chance to investigate the whole thing. And word to that effect to the Senator and Shannahan."

Hosty pulled a handkerchief from his pocket and mopped his face, despite the sharp chill in the air.

"Whew! he grunted. "That sure spoils things—or would, if it had a chance!"

"Looks to me like it does. Even if Gertney gets back, he can't go ahead against orders. If'n he did that, he'd face criminal charges, and I don't reckon he'd want to risk that. Not from the Federal Goverment."

147

Hosty was thinking fast. Now he took his decision.

"Thanks for tellin' me," he said. "Keep me posted on anything that comes up—but *keep this under your hat!* Gertney don't know it yet—and if he don't find it out, official, till after he's taken action—then nobody can blame him any more'n they could before!"

Not stopping to answer questions, he got his horse and led a score of picked men afield. Seeing them coming, Shannahan watched dejectedly. He'd hoped to get to friends—or to army men, at least. This had the look of defeat.

Hosty's actions did nothing to allay his suspicion of the man. He took charge of both, having them put on horseback as gently as possible. His solicitude for Shannahan seemed to be equal to that for Gertney. But he made it plain that he was taking charge.

"We'll take you back to the post, Shannahan," he said. "That's where you belong, havin' broken out of jail. I wouldn't think of interferin' with the army. As for Gertney, he's my friend, and I'll look after him."

He was as good as his word, delivering Shannahan to the sentry at the gate, then going on into town with Gertney. The latter was still despondent. Here at least was rescue from the thing he had most dreaded because it seemed most imminent, but to him the situation seemed hopeless.

"Everything's spoiled," he said sourly. "Thanks to Shannahan. Why the devil did you turn him back to the post?" he added with a flash of his old asperity. "I'd have liked to settle with him."

"He won't do no harm there," Hosty assured him. "And I'm doing everything so that'll look like we're working' with the

148

authorities. Do you want the news—or not?"

"Why not? It can't be any worse than it is."

"Well, all I'm tellin' you is a rumor that I've heard—so that sure ain't official," Hosty cautioned, and gave the Washington news to him. Then he grinned. "But we ain't licked yet, eh?"

"How do you figure that?" Gertney demanded, amazed. "My hands are tied. I'm sick."

"But not too sick to open the reservation, official, yet this afternoon. I'll start the word around that you'll do it. And I'll take mighty good care that the agent don't deliver any messages to you, so you won't hear anything—official."

Gertney stared, then the hope faded and he shook his head.

"It's too late," he said. "Shannahan's a slippery devil. He'll find some way to stop us. If you'd held on to him—"

"What can he do? What can anyone do? We've got force on our side—and we'll use it! I got as big a stake in this as you have, remember. The army's out in the hills. They won't get back till long after dark, at the earliest. It'll be done by then. And once it's started, nothing can stop it! You'll have plenty witnesses that you never got the Secretary's message till after you'd acted!"

Excitement flared in Gertney's face. Here was the sort of thing he liked—success, revenge all rolled into one, at the last moment. Snatching victory from defeat.

"I didn't promise Shannahan that I wouldn't try to take any sort of action," he muttered. "Still, a promise made under duress—"

"Your word ain't worth a damn, and never was, so that don't worry you any," Hosty reminded him bluntly. "I'll tell the boys to spread the word that the land will be thrown open at four this afternoon. And by then I'll have a thousand men behind me, if Shannahan tries to interfere. Nothin' short of the army could bother—and they're too far away! Right?''

"Go to it, Gertney agreed savagely. "We'll make a killing—and I mean killing, before it's finished!''

Chapter Eight

DESPAIR TOUCHED Shannahan as he was turned over to the sentry at the gate. That act voiced the complete confidence of Hosty that the situation was now under his control. Up to then, Shannahan had hoped. Now he understood the enemy's plans as well as if they had been explained. With everyone gone, they'd take one last gamble, rushing the opening that same day. And with overwhelming force on their side, it looked unbeatable. The fact that the army was far afield made all the difference.

The corporal of the guard, called to take charge of the prisoner, was puzzled. Here was the man for whom the whole army was hunting, an escaped prisoner. As such, his disposition should have been simple enough, back to the guard house. But Corporal MacVeigh was a shrewd man and inclined to caution. He had over-heard only that morning, a snatch of conversation between the Major and the Senator, before they rode away to lead the search.

Words enough to make it plain to MacVeigh that this

151

Shannahan was a personal friend of the senator, and that Reardon was greatly interested in his welfare. And it was no light matter to bundle the friend of a United States Senator into the guardhouse.

MacVeigh's dilemma was solved by the appearance of Kate. She exclaimed at sight of Shannahan, his bearded, fatigue-line face, and promptly gave instructions for assisting him to her house, which was also the Major's. She bade the corporal to fetch the doctor also, as speedily as possible.

Not until Shannahan was inside, however, deep sunk in a chair with both Kate and Dot fussing over him, did she stop to ask questions.

"We'll have some dinner for you in a jiffy," she assured him. "You look as if you'd had a terrible time."

"If I'd known this was the sort of a guard house I'd be returned to, I'd have come back sooner." Shannahan managed a grin, but his eyes followed her with a light in them which set Kate's pulses beating at an unaccustomed rate. "I didn't suppose the army was chasin' me because it was quite so solicitous of my welfare."

"Your friend Senator Reardon is here, and he's riding with my brother today, leading the search," Kate explained. For the next few minutes they were very busy, filling in the main gaps of news since Shannahan's dramatic departure from Antelope.

"Kate thinks you're a rather wonderful man," Dot said suddenly, the first suspicion of a smile in many days hovering about her mouth. "And I guess I'll have to agree with her. I don't know who else could have played with the army, such a

152

game of hide and seek, and fooled them.''

"That was as much luck as anything else,'' Shannahan disclaimed, then further conversation was interrupted by the arrival of the doctor. He was a little bird-like man with positive ideas on many subjects, who had chosen the army for his field because he disliked the confines of conventional practice. Having asked a few questions and made his examination, removing the lariat rope for the first time since Shannahan had fixed it in place, he smiled and gave his verdict.

"You have five cracked ribs, which, thanks to a constitution like a horse and the heroic treatment you imposed upon yourself, are doing as well as can be expected. Aside from abrasions and soreness, there's nothing much wrong with you that a few good meals and sleep won't cure. Though I would advise a less strenuous program for the next couple of weeks. Just as a matter of comfort, of course; necessity is a much abused word, and we won't drag it in where it would feel out of place.''

He stood up briskly, then turned back at the door as an afterthought.

"Rather too bad, after what you've gone through, to lose out on your fight. As an officer, I have no opinions. As a medico, I've been hoping that you'd win out, Mr. Shannahan. It's a shame, this throwing open the reservation to settlement at four o'clock this afternoon.''

Shannahan came to his feet. This was the sort of thing he had feared, but confirmation was like a blow.

"What's that?'' he exclaimed. "Tell me about it.''

The doctor shrugged.

153

"All I know is that Rees Hosty is spreadin' the word that the drawing will be at four this afternoon, with the staking right after. The town's gone mad."

Kate cried out sharply. Dorothy stood, her face bloodless. Unlike Shannahan, they had not forseen this. Kate knew enough of the sentiment in her brother's heart, particularly since the arrival of the Senator, to feel that he would not permit such high-handed action, even if interference might get him into trouble.

The orderly knocked on the door.

"Telegrams," he said. "For Senator Reardon and Mr. Shannahan."

Shannahan read his own quickly. Here was victory—and confirmation of what he had expected.

"They're taking good care that Gertney doesn't get his—officially, at least," he grunted. "They'll see to that if they have to shoot the agent to stop him from delivering it. Tomorrow he can hand it over—after the job is done! They've got overwhelming force on their side, and they aim to use it!"

"But there must be something—some way—" Dot said hopelessly. "After this—"

"The difficulty is that the army's out of town—and Gertney's taking advantage of it," Shannahan said grimly, and clutched at the back of a chair to steady himself. "If there was only some way to get them back in time! Force, and law, is the only thing that Gertney will respect now. But—four o'clock! He's timed it nicely. He knows perfectly well that they won't return before dark, which will be too late. It would take until four for a man on horseback to even reach them!"

"In any case, you're not the man to ride that horse and try and find them," Kate assured him. "Sit down and eat. It's ready, and that's what you need first."

Shannahan sank into the chair, frowning. This was bitter medicine, to be faced with defeat after all that he had done, and with victory in sight. It would be hopeless to try and reach Gertney with official news. They'd be on guard against any such attempt.

The army would be back before morning, but hours too late. Everything hinged on the next few hours.

Shannahan had seen the men in blue ride out, missing him by miles. He knew just about where they would be now, knew that it was too far for even a fast horseman to reach them and get the word for them to beat the deadline back.

"Have you any idea where Bob LaFontise is?" he inquired.

"He's out in the hills, too, this afternoon, looking for the Major," Kate explained. "He came here and said he had some important news for Mike, and he didn't say what it was. Then he started out."

That meant one more slim hope gone. LaFontise could do much, if there was any chance at all. Shannahan ate mechanically, then laid down his knife and fork. Kate was close to tears.

"Oh, there must be *something* that we can do," she wailed. "After all you've done. Bob will be with them by now, of course. But that doesn't help any."

Shannahan had to agree with her. Whatever news LaFontise might have for the Major, it wasn't likely to alter McLeod's plans for keeping on with the search as long as they could see. Then he came to his feet, almost oversetting his chair. He clutched at it again to keep from falling.

"I'm so damned weak!" he said savagely. "But if he's with them—there's a chance! He's an Indian, and proud of it—proud of the old tribal lore. The air is clear today. We can't see them, because we don't know where to look, back in the timber and deep in the hills. But from where they'll be, high up they can see us—the town and the post, well enough!"

Both girls were watching him, struck by the sudden excitement in his voice.

"What then?" Dot breathed.

"Smoke signals!" Shannahan said triumphantly. "The kind the Indians used in the old days before the white man came. To send a message across the miles, faster than the fastest horse could run! I know how they do it, the proper way to send a message to get them back here on the double-quick! And Bob can read the smokes. If only I wasn't so infernally weak—"

"Never mind about that!" Kate was beside him, her eyes shining, easing him back into his chair. "You go ahead and eat your dinner. Dot and I can build the fires, with some of the men to help us. You tell us how to send the smoke!" She flung open the door, beckoned imperiously for the sentry.

"Order every available man to bring piles of wood on to the parade ground at the double-quick!" she exclaimed. "This is a message to the army! Hurry!"

The sentry hurried. Strictly speaking, this was a highly unorthodox proceeding, with all the commanding officers absent, and this order being given by a slip of a girl. But she was the Major's sister, and there was not a man on the post who would

156

not cheerfully have died for her, had she asked him to. In this, which was plainly an emergency, he'd run the risk, and willingly, of taking orders from Kate McLeod.

"Some green boughs will be needed, to make plenty of smoke, and a couple of blankets," Shannahan instructed. "I'll help with the blankets myself as soon as things are ready." He turned to wolf his food, grinning. "This is something that Gertney, Hosty and Company won't be counting on."

"And if our boys look this way and see the signals soon, then ride like the devil, they may get here by the deadline!" Kate exclaimed, and was quite unconscious that her phraseology patterned closely after her brother's in such a moment of stress.

GERTNEY'S SPIRITS revived fast. From being completely at the nadir he soared to the zenith as preparations went forward. The station agent had attempted to deliver the telegram from Gertney's superior, but various subordinates had frustrated the attempt, doing it in such a way that Gertney would be supposed to have no knowledge of it.

A doctor, called from town, had pronounced him in excellent shape, considering what he had been through. The wounded leg was healing in fine fashion. All that he needed was food and rest. Now, with the hour set, the town swarming with men who would cheer his name to the echo if given a cause to do so, Gertney was elated.

With the army out of town, he could see nothing which could stop him. There was no other adequate force at hand. Once the

157

rush had started, nothing could check it or undo the work. He took a savage pleasure in that knowledge, as well as in the fact that men like Mead, the railroad king, would pay him well because it could not be stopped.

Tomorrow he would receive the telegram from his boss. His action then would be a letter of explanation and regret, along with his resignation. Nobody could touch him. The fact that he had been kidnapped and subjected to all sorts of indignities during the past several days would, however unreasonably from the precise point of fact, be a strong argument in his favor. A lot of public opinion would be on his side.

He was safe enough in what he was doing. More to the point, his profits were assured.

Replete with a good meal, buoyed by such comfortable reflections, he found it not too difficult to walk, using a pair of crutches. He came to a window and stared out at the town, bustling with activity as men prepared frantically for the race to stake which would come later in the day. Something caught his eye, and he looked more closely, then watched with strained attention where smoke rose in irregular puffs toward the sky. This day, for a wonder, there was no wind, and no cloud in the sky. The smoke rose up straight as permitted, high and easy to see.

"Hosty!" Gertney bellowed, and waved an arm madly. Still clutching a crutch, his wild gesture shattered one of the window panes, but he scarcely noticed as Hosty came running, his face gone suddenly bloodless at the agitation in his fellow-conspirator's voice.

"What is it?" he croaked. "Somethin' wrong?"

"There's hell and all to pay," Gertney roared. "Look there!"

"Looks like smoke," he said. "Out at the post. Somethin' afire, maybe?"

"You dumb fool," Gertney said witheringly. "Don't you know what that is? That's Indian smoke talk." He controlled himself with an effort, remembering that Hosty probably could not read such a message. Few white men could. But Gertney, though he had a vast contempt for the people placed under the care of his department, understood smoke talk. He could read those puffs as precisely as a printed page.

"They're signalin' the army," he grated. "Telling them there's trouble and to get back here on the double-quick! That's Shannahan's doings again. You idiot offspring of a long line of numbskulls! You had to take him back to the fort, didn't you, instead of keeping him where we could watch him!"

Hosty stared with sagging jaw as the significance became manifest. For a moment he thought wildly of trying to stop them from sending up more smoke, but as quickly abandoned the notion. Not only was it too late, for already the smoke would have been see. But even he was not reckless enough to consider leading an outlaw crew on to an army post and attempting by force to overpower the few soldiers there. He could muster sufficient force to do it, but retribution would be swift.

Instead, like Gertney, he turned to look at the big clock on a shelf, at the pointing hands.

"Mebby—mebby they won't be able to get back here before

159

four," he hazarded, and ran a furry tongue across suddenly dry lips.

"There's no need of being a bigger fool than nature intended, Hosty," Gertney said, and some quality in the words, the very quietness of them, stopped further argument. "They'll be here. We've lost, and we might as well face it. Even if we tried to start the drawing, they'd come busting in right in the middle, and hell would let loose. They'd hang us before it was over."

"But we've told that crowd that the land'll be opened at four," Hosty reminded. "They've been cheated once, as they figure. If we don't do it, *they'll* lynch us—and I don't mean maybe!"

"I was thinking about that," Gertney said. "That, and other things. We're both in this together, Hosty."

Hosty was thinking of that too—unhappily. This meant that they had a couple of hours leeway. A couple of hours in which to get out of town, to get a start and keep ahead of both the law and the lawless. If either caught up, it would be just too bad.

Both had been willing to risk everything when victory seemed probable. To the victors belong the spoils. It was an ancient adage, and however trite, they liked the truth which could be squeezed out of it. Even an opponent is generally willing, often anxious, to change sides, to attached himself to the bandwagon of the victor. With success, money, power, the crowd on their side, they could defy the law.

But in failure, even the crimes which they had only tried to commit would be held against them, sufficient to destroy them. Their only salvation lay in flight.

"I'm glad we're in this together," Gertney went on, and his words were biting. "It's your fault that we're licked, Hosty —your bungling. But because we'll hang separately if we don't stick together, you'll help me get away. And I'll make it worth your while. I've got a lot of money cached away against such an evil day."

"Sure, I'll help you," Hosty agreed readily. This was no time for argument.

"And before we go, there's one chore that has to be tended to," Gertney reminded softly. "Shannahan's done this. He's got to die."

"Think I'd go without that?" Hosty demanded. This was one matter on which he was in full agreement. He was thinking hard. "I'll get things ready—a buggy to travel in, an' so on. But how are we going to get at Shannahan? We can't reach him at the post."

"I've been studying about that," Gertney said. "He'll know he's won, now. That will make a difference. They all figure that way, and that they're safe. Look there!"

He pointed to where someone rode a horse, at the far end of the street, heading toward the heart of town. Dot Hauswirth.

"She's sure that everything is all right," he added. "Get her in here—with as little disturbance as possible, but get her!"

Hosty gave him a scared look.

"You had her grabbed once," he pointed out. "But that was different. They might figure you was back of it, but—"

Gertney cut him short, contemptuously.

"She won't be hurt," he said. "Unless you bungle. As for

161

the rest, who cares? If they ever catch us, they'll lynch us anyway. But she'll bring Shannahan here. Jump!''

Hosty obeyed. With almost equal promptness a message went out to Shannahan—a terse message in Gertney's own florid scrawl.

"I want to talk to you, Shannahan, and I want to do it now. Come to the Powder Horn. Whether Dot Hauswirth ever sees another day or not depends on your answer. If you come now, she goes free. That's one promise I'll keep, because I've no further interest in her. As proof, she can go out as you come in."

Shannahan, studying the message a few minutes later, had a feeling that it meant exactly what it said. Kate watched him with anxious eyes.

''But it's a trap,'' she protested. ''And it's you they're after. Besides, he never keeps a promise.''

''He'll keep this so far as she is concerned,'' Shannahan decided. ''We made a mistake, letting her go into town. As it is—well, he means it. Either way, he'll keep it so far as she is concerned.''

Kate shivered. She knew how Mike felt regarding Dorothy, and her own feeling toward her was that of a sister. They hadn't foreseen such a trick, with Gertney turning Shannahan's own ruse against him. This was a dreadful game, now being played to its final, inevitable end.

''I—I don't know what to tell you,'' she whispered. ''I suppose you have to go. But I—I'm afraid, Sam.''

162

He did not confess that he too, was afraid. This was playing the other man's game, and he had no illusions as to who the trap was set for. Yet he could do no other. He knew what Dot meant to the Major, and hope was in him that Mike McLeod might one day be his own brother-in-law. In any case Dunk Hauswirth had been his friend, and he'd asked Shannahan to look out for Dorothy.

"There's no one who can be sent from here with you," Kate said. "I want you to—to come back to me, Sam."

"I aim to come," he said quietly. And, seeing what was in her eyes, knowing what might lie ahead, he reached and took her in his arms. He could feel her trembling, feel the long promise of her kiss before he released her. But now he was smiling.

"With you to come back to," he said. "I can't fail, Kate."

It had been simple, in town. So easy, getting the girl inside the building, that a new idea had come to Hosty, born of hate. Gertney would be only an encumberance if he had to take him along, a drag on his own chances. And it was Gertney whom the crowd and the law alike would hate, once deadline was behind them, merged in fresh disappointment and frustration.

Gertney had promised him excellent pay from a hidden hoard of money, if he helped him escape. Hosty had no doubt that Gertney had the money. Neither did he have the slightest notion that he would ever lay hands on a penny of it, if he once succeeded in getting the man to safety. A promise was a cheap coin to Gertney.

Now Hosty saw how easily things could be done. If kidnapping, why not murder? He hated Shannahan, who had ruined all

163

his plans. But this hatred for Gertney was almost equal. The words which Gertney had employed, dubbing him a fool and a bungler, still burned in his mind. Searing words, such as he could never have phrased and the more biting on that account.

To take Gertney would mean sharing his guilt and doubling the danger. But if Gertney was left behind—left in such a way that all thought and attention would be centered there, and so distracted from himself, the guilt found all in one room—then he'd have nothing to fear.

It was the difference between life and death, and doubly pleasant since the life would be his own, death would come to Gertney and Shannahan.

There was one factor which Gertney had overlooked. That the Powder Horn was Hosty's saloon, his stronghold. There were secrets connected with it not known to outsiders. Professional secrets in a manner of speaking.

Hurrying back inside, Hosty's mind was busy with details. So much so that he failed completely to notice an Indian across the street. In any case, he would have paid no attention. This was the reservation town, and Indians were so common that he regarded them with contempt, solely as a source of profit for rotgut whiskey.

THEY WERE OBSERVING the first part of the agreement with meticulous nicety. Dot Hauswirth came out to the street at a sidedoor as Shannahan reached the front, and she hurried away while someone still apologized profusely. Probably she had no real inkling of the part she had played, of the real drama just beginning to unfold.

164

Shannahan entered the big saloon. A bar-tender, recognizing him, jerked a thumb toward a stairs.

"Right up there," he said. It was all as casual as though this was an every-day sort of appointment, not a rendezvous with death. Shannahan had no doubt as to what waited, merely the form which it would take. Now that Dorothy was out on the street again, he might have swung back. Two things prevented, equally potent.

He'd come, and Gertney counted on him to go through with a job, once he'd started. Even such a job as this. Also there would be watchers posted, out of sight. Men with instructions to drop him if he failed to come ahead.

What would wait in one of the rooms upstairs was to be discovered. Gertney would be there. There was no doubt in Shannahan's mind, for Gertney would not want to miss any of this. But whether he would be content to try and settle it, man to man—on that hinged, for him, the rising of the morrow's sun.

Shannahan paused at the top of the stairs, getting his breath. It hurt to climb, and the nagging pain must be slowed before he could hope to slap leather in a contest with Gertney or any other man. He utilized the few moments of grace to study his surroundings, for this was the other man's set-up, and that counted heavily. There was not much to see. A long hall, between closed doors, with a window at the far end. Part way down a door stood open.

He reached it paused again, and here the light was better. The rays of the afternoon sun slanted through a window on the opposite wall and set small dust motes agleam like fragments of rainbows. It was a bare room, the walls smoothly white, the

165

floor boards scuffed and uneven. Completely empty, save for a chair near one corner. In that sat Gertney, his injured leg propped before him, across a box which served as stool. A revolver lay in his lap.

"So you came," he nodded to Shannahan. "I thought you would."

Shannahan closed the door, keeping his eyes on Gertney. There was a key in the lock, and he turned it.

"You said you wanted to talk." he suggested.

"That was just to get you here, and you knew it," Gertney grunted. "The time to talk between us is past, Shannahan. You've won, damn you—ruining all my plans, spoiling as sweet a set-up as I've ever run across. So now I'm going to kill you. You've got a gun and you can have your try as well. I almost hope you succeed, the way things are. But I'm going to take you with me."

It looked to be on the level. An even break, which in its way was not so much to be wondered at. Gertney had been a gunman in his day. But that day was overgrown by a tissue of fat times and slovenliness, and the speed which once had been in his hand was there no longer. It was that which made Shannahan suspect a trap, and he could see no sign of it. Gertney was speaking again.

"I'm going to count to three," he said. "And at three I'm going to kill you. That's all I have to say. One—"

It was a soft sound, as compared to a gun-shot—just a thudding noise, curiously muted. Commotion followed. A section of the apparently solid wall tore with a ripping sound, and Rees Hosty fell through, sprawling full length on the floor in

166

front of them. A revolver was clutched in his hand, and he still held it clasped as he fell and rolled half over.

As he lay, it was easy to see the manner of his death—an arrow, still quivering, driven deep between the shoulder-blades, straight to the heart.

Startled, Shannahan saw the trick. This was Hosty's saloon, and like Gertney he was a man who lived by trickery. That section of wall had been a sheet of cloth stretched taut, covered on this side like the wall with a coat of paint, so that it would take foreknowledge as well as a keen eye to detect it.

But standing on the opposite side of the sheet; with the sunlight slanting through, Hosty had been able to see into this room. So that he could shoot when he chose, and there would be no risk for Gertney. Hosty was to do the shooting, probably at the count of two.

Gertney stared at the arrow, his face gone flabby. He seemed to have forgotten the gun in his lap. Something stirred in the empty space behind the torn wall, and Straight Arrow, the grandfather of Bob LaFontise, stood there. A man who had ranged widely and fought his battles before the signing of the treaty.

A bow and arrow, slack now, were in his right hand. He looked through the torn wall and bowed, with the courtliness of his French ancestry, toward the three men in the room, the living and the dead.

"Long time ago, Running Deer, my friend, Running Deer come home to die," he said. "He left for dead outside this place. Shot up here. He tell me about wall which is no wall."

He gestured, and there was a gleam of contempt in his eyes as they flitted from the fallen Hosty to the pasty-faced Gertney.

"Little while ago, I see Shannahan go in saloon. Then I see Hosty go up, by outside stair, in a window. Straight Arrow remember Running Deer. Follow, watch at window, hear Hosty talk."

His glance shifted to Gertney, and there was amusement in it now, a sly derisive quality worse than contempt.

"Hosty say to himself, *you* expect him kill Shannahan. But *he* aim to let Shannahan kill you, *then* he shoot Shannahan, make look like you kill each other."

Straight Arrow was silent, allowing time for Gertney to understand. One bullet, fired through the sheet, would have left no noticeable mark.

"But you and Hosty both like snake—strike without warning," Straight Arrow went on. "Too much risk. Shannahan fight for Indian—for reservation. It only fair that Indian help white brother to keep treaty like *honest* white men and Indian intend—as long as grass grows."

"Thanks, Straight Arrow," Shannahan said. "I won't forget." He turned to Gertney. "You've still got your gun in your lap."

Sound beat at them, across the town. A medley made up of many emotions. Part of it was cheering, a part was disappointment as others realized that deadline had come and gone. The army was back.

Gertney started and swung half around, listening. He turned back then, and his gaze on Shannahan held naked hate. But defeat was there as well, a flabbiness of soul matched by the outward body. He looked down at the gun in his lap, staring as if

168

he would force his hand to try for it. He did move a little —sufficiently that the weapon slid and dropped to the floor.

"What's left to fight about, Shannahan?" he asked hoarsely. "You've won."

Straight Arrow had already departed, slipping down to the street. Not bothering to reply, not even glancing toward the broken man in the chair, Shannahan turned and unlocked the door and walked out and down the stairs. Men watched him go, but no one made a move to detain him. Out in the street again, he filled his lungs with the clean air, glancing up to the false balcony and the outer stairs which climbed to it, to that second window fronting on a room made for murder.

It was as he crossed the street that a gun thundered again from the second floor, one echoing blast. Gertney had turned in his resignation.

From where he walked, Shannahan saw Mike McLeod spurring, dignity thrown to the winds. Then he was up with Dot Hauswirth and swinging from his horse, catching her in his arms as she gave way to a storm of tears.

Just behind him, tall and straight in the saddle, rode Bob LaFontise. He saw Straight Arrow and dismounted. The old man nodded and smiled and put his hand on his grandson's shoulder.

"You have learned many things in the east, my son, but it is well that you have not forgotten the lore of our people." He waved his arm for Shannahan to approach. "You are friends and will remain so, and that is good, for working together, you will keep our land happy."

A commotion swept through the crowd as a rider tore recklessly through, her hair streaming in the wind. Shannahan turned and his eyes lighted up. Kate McLeod dismounted and rushed toward him, and he hurried in turn, forgetful of his ribs. In any case, if he remembered right, wives and ribs had an old affinity in common.